AM I STILL LAUGHING?

By

DOLLY SEN

FOR MUM

Published by:
Chipmukapublishing
PO Box 6872
Brentwood
Essex
CM13 1ZT
United Kingdom

www.chipmunkapublishing.com

ISBN 978 1 905610 94

Cover photo: Melanie Clifford
Back cover photo: Magali Moreau

Acknowledgements

Thanks to Jason Pegler for his continued friendship and support; thanks to all at Creative Routes; thanks to Barry Fitton and Karen Francis for being angels that have made my path more interesting; love to my family, especially the newest additions Hannah-Marie and Kallum; eternal thanks to my wonderful and beautiful friend Melanie Clifford; biggest love and thanks goes to the woman who endlessly inspires my soul and taught me to love totally, Sarah Tonin.

Not forgetting my 4-legged muses – Cupasoup, Pot Noodle, Gem, Mr Cat, Mungo, Coco, Ty, and Miroslav, and Lux.

The development of this book was made possible by a grant from The Arts Council, London.

IN MEMORY OF PETE SHAUGHNESSY
Sept 1962 – Dec 2002

'Epur si muove'- 'and yet it does move' were the famous words supposedly uttered by Galileo at the end of his trial for heresy when the Inquisition told him that the sun is immoveable and the centre of the world.

Dolly's book is a chronicle of a life made up of uncomfortable truths. The issues she raises are written with words that evoke mind spinning, dancing emotions and will challenge you to telescope your inner self.

She is an exhilarating mad astronaut probing the frontiers of our realities, writing in a down to earth way as she chronicles despair, tears, abuse and the beauty of mad power, whilst circling above on her pink hated flying dog, hurling insane laughter on a world that however hard it tries not to hear – must.

The Royal College of Psychiatry should pulp all their books and read this if they are ever to really understand madness.

'All truths are easy to understand once they are discovered; the point is to discover them.' Galileo

Dolly you are the centre of my world

SarahGem Tonin, Creative Routes
Mad Astronauts United

INTRODUCTION

For those of you who haven't read my first memoir 'The World is Full of Laughter', here is a quick summary:
I say of it, it started as a possible suicide note but ended as a celebration of life. The book begins with me with a knife in my hand, wanting to kill my father. This was the end point of suffering years of horrific abuse from him, and also the worst point of my mental illness, which I am sure the abuse contributed towards creating. I thought I had come to the end point of my life, but something happened. I realised I *could* kill my father, but I also eventually realised I didn't have to, that in fact I could have an amazing life. It was a matter of changing my thinking from negativity to positivity. The book detailed my childhood and subsequent mental illness, and my life up to 2002, when I was 31. It is a dark book at times, but always injected with a wry humour.

I ended the World is Full of Laughter on a positive note, brimming and shining with optimism for the future. It has been three years since that book was written, am I now as positive and optimistic as I was then? Am I still laughing? How is my mental health now? How has my life changed? What has happened to my dad and the rest of my family?

Well, it's amazing what can happen in three years, and I *am* a changed person from the one who wrote the book.

There is one obvious difference about this book compared to the last one. There is going to be less focus on my father and more on me. That's what letting go means, you are not fixated on one person to the exclusion of everyone – and everything - else. And what a feeling of release it is to let go of some of the anger and hatred. My life feels lighter now, there is more room for myself and other people. And I am astonished how many people are now in my life. When you hate someone, you are giving them far too much of yourself, far too much of your thoughts, your soul, your body and emotions to them. Aren't your thoughts, soul, body, emotion yours? When you hate someone you let them own so much of your soul and time. My father now, out of a combination of just getting older, progressive dementia, seeing that his aggression and controlling attitude will get him nowhere, and reduced access to alcohol, has turned into something of a pussycat... most of the time. He comes around occasionally to spend time with the family and to watch TV, and I marvel at the change in the man. I remember being a small child and seeing him as a huge brute of a man – which he was then – and being under that powerful flesh avalanche of his punches and kicks. But now I see him sitting in the armchair, a withered old man, scared, very scared. His memory is going so I know the world for him is frightening and confusing at times; time doesn't give new memories, it just takes away more of them. He will reread the day's newspaper again and again and everything will be fresh news to him. He will reminisce of things that never happened. It is somewhat of a blessing for him. He doesn't remember what a bastard he was, or the vile things he did to us. His memory of my childhood is a happy, carefree one. I guess it is not really a blessing, if you don't realise you've forgotten something horrible. Because if you don't have that memory, it never happened, nothing to feel blessed that you have forgotten.

But I haven't forgotten.

But I have just about forgiven.

May 2002

After years of sitting alone, suffering in silence, razor-whipped, razor-jarred by negativity and isolation, I decided to take small steps into improving the quality of my life. I started by doing voluntary work and visiting free galleries and museums.

As I gained more confidence I went out more. One Thursday morning, I would have rather have stayed in and watched TV, my energy levels were quite low and my attention span almost non-existent, but as per usual when I felt like this, I pushed myself off the sofa and out through the front door. Usually on a Thursday I went to LUV's weekly Coffee Morning. LUV was Lambeth User Voice, a forum for mental health service users to support each other amongst other things. I enjoyed talking with the regulars there, Barry, Andrew and John. Carole Myers, the user development worker for LUV, used to laugh at my stories. This time she wasn't there but there was a new face around the table. I took off my coat and this new face stuck out his hand for me to shake. "My name's Jason." "Dolly," I smiled back. There was a book in front of him. I compared the guy on the cover with Jason and realised they were the same person. "You wrote a book?" "Yeah, I published it too." "Really, wow, I'm a writer and publisher too." "Really? Wow." We talked shop and exchanged email addresses. I had no idea that it would be one of the defining turning points of my life.

We emailed each other for a while, talking about writing mostly before I got his book 'A Can of Madness' in the post. I read the book straight through, and then read it again. It blew me away. I had read books like

'The Bell Jar' with great curiosity because they talked about the 'mad' experience. Now I had met an author of a 'mad memoir' in the flesh, and he didn't kill himself but was remarkably positive. He wanted to change the world and how it viewed mad people. I had been planning my own memoir in my head for years. I began to write seriously in 1992 when I was 21, and my memoir was in my plans then but I kept putting it off with other literary projects because I was basically too scared to do it. I thought it would be so painful, that it would turn into a suicide note. Jason really inspired me to finally sit down and write my story, so that's what I did. Once I actually started it, the story couldn't be stopped, it wanted to be told. I spent about 12 hours a day on the computer, with lots of necessary breaks to chill out. It was bittersweet liberation. I felt freed by the writing of my life but also I don't think I had cried so much in my life. It was like watching a speed aging of a scared, scarred child into a scared, scarred adult. I wanted a happy ending for this person, and writing the book gave me an opportunity to script a better future for me.

Writing has always helped me. I found it when I was 22 and it has kept me alive since then. During my worst depressions, writing gave me a reason to wake up in the morning. Would I still have carried on writing if I never was published? Of course I would. One of my favourite writers, Charles Bukowski, said of writing: 'It is the last expectation, the last explanation, that's what writing is'. A plain piece of paper won't judge you, criticize you. And above all it won't lie to you. If you can't say what needs to be said face to face, write it down.

People with mental health problems who are able should think about either writing their story or at least telling it. Their lives shouldn't be what they think are dirty secrets they have to hide. One woman at one of my book signings shook her head sadly and said, "I can't, it's too painful. And besides, nobody wants to hear it." That's what I thought once. I now know that to be untrue. People, men and women, young and old, rich and poor, have taken me aside after reading my book and say, sometimes with tears in their eyes, "This happened to me too... but please don't tell anyone that it did." This is painfully heart-rending. Because I think if you don't share it positively, it'll manifest somewhere else, in your body, in your relationship to others and the world. For example, it can be seen in some people's eyes; they try to smile, but their eyes don't believe it. Their eyes are telling their story – something about their life always will. So you might as well have some control over it.

For me creativity gave me control in a world where because of a diagnosis I had no control. A South American poet said, "Take away someone's creativity and you take away their humanity. Give someone back their creativity, and you give back their life." I found this to be true while writing my story, and every day after too.

Writing your life story does so much for you. It gives you opportunity to reflect, it empowers you because you have nothing to hide any more.
I made a conscious decision to let it out, to give away secrets. But it was really difficult to get it onto paper sometimes without crying; or deleting, starting again, deleting, and starting again. Some of the things I wrote

I didn't tell my family about. Most of them didn't know about the abortion or the extent of my mental illness.

Will they reject me for what needs to be said? That did definitely cross my mind. I even made plans to leave London if things got ugly. The first to read it was Paula. When she finished it, she rang me up in tears. "Why didn't you tell me? About the abortion and other things? Oh Dolly..." So we cried together. I was so relieved that she didn't reject me; in fact, it made our relationship stronger. This goes with the other members of my family too. Our love got stronger. It dumbfounded me. Of course, my father won't read it – or can't. His memory is such that he doesn't remember what he reads. For example, he will read the same newspaper 5 or 6 times without retaining information. And nothing can change the story he tells himself anyway. Jason was intuitively supportive, just knowing exactly the right time to encourage me. His belief in me was nothing I had from anyone in my life previously. I remember thinking this is the thing that all humans need, the thing that affect change in someone, no matter what has happened in their life before. I am forever grateful for him for that. And because of his belief in me, my self-belief developed slowly.

So I didn't get to see much of the summer of 2002. I had spent most of it, sweating inside, writing the book. When it was finished, I felt like a new person, my skin was easier to wear. The thing I thought would be the hardest thing to do was in fact very uplifting and life-refreshing. I felt I could do anything... until I realised how much my life would now change. Being a published writer, I had to engage with people, talk to them! And talk in front of them! I was shitting myself. I wanted to go back and hide, not unwrite the book but be anonymous again. As the publication date loomed closer and closer, Jason gave me things to do to occupy myself. He needed photos for the book cover, so I got my brother Kenny to emerge from behind his computers and take some pics of me with his digital camera. "What are they for?" he asked. "Oh, they are for the cover of my new book." "Oh right, I see." Like it was something we did everyday. But Kenny is used to my craziness. If I said, Kenny we have to burn socks so the devil doesn't have fossil fuel. He would have said, "Oh right, I see."

I wanted the picture on the front cover to confuse the reader, to contradict the title 'The World is Full of Laughter'. So I sat under the haunting light of the living room window, with my arms wrapped around my knees, and looked reflectively into the distance. The back cover also needed a photo, so we made that one more upbeat, to show that the world can indeed be full of laughter, with my arms outstretched to welcome the world with a grin on my face. Jason also wanted me to find a quote to put on the front of the book, but in the end we decided to use the one he had on his: 'one million people a year commit suicide', a staggering statistic, and a reminder why Chipmunka is an essential enterprise, better to have our stories than our suicide notes.

The book launch was set for October 19th 2002 at the Lavender Pub in Vauxhall. The day got closer, and my stomach tightened. I was just on the jittery cusp of total anonymity and recognition, my brain and soul couldn't settle in my skin. I was losing sleep and wanting to hide. The thing I wanted and dreamed about and yearned for, of being published, was doing my head in. I was scared, I couldn't conceal myself any longer. After being ignored most of my life, I was used to it, being lonely and anonymous was my comfort zone, funnily enough. I now had to be the centre of attention, and it was unnerving.

I did almost chicken out of making that step out of obscurity, but I knew if I did I would regret, I would be constantly thinking, 'What if? What if? I had to trust my strength. We all have strength, it is whether we use it. It is forbidding, no doubt about it.

I didn't sleep the night before. I wrote a speech. But I hoped no-one would ask me to read it. I hoped I could hide at my own book launch!
My sisters, Mum and a couple of friends came with me to the pub. Jason saw I was nervous and gave me a smile. In his arms was a box of my books. He opened them and let me survey them. I felt a flush of pride that I had come this far: I hadn't written a suicide note but a book people were going to read.

Everyone at the book launch was mostly Jason's friends and associates. And they were lovely and supportive. A few of them were from Mad Pride, and they were the most vital, interesting and funny people there. Ben Watson gave me encouragement and promised to write a review, which he did later on. Rob Dellar was particularly amazing. Some people have 'it', that makes them stand out from the crowd and Rob had it. He ran Spare Change books which published Mad Pride books. I ran Hole Books which published my books and other books dealing with social issues such as the Death Penalty, and we did a swap of books. He had a huge heart and I felt it. So the night wasn't so bad, after all. In fact, it was ecstatic, it was triumphant. My body was as light as feather, my soul the reason it could fly. I could have copped out and stayed home, stayed in my comfort zone, and not pushed myself. But I realised that day: do I want to stay stuck and not go beyond this stuckness? Can I move beyond? I pushed myself and proved that I could. I felt my soul being refreshed as it now had brand new air to breathe and not the stale air of my fear and conditioned self-hate.

I was on a high for days afterwards, and feeling good about myself helped fuel a momentum of pushing myself in my life. During the summer an ad in the Big Issue caught my eye. The King's Fund, a charity aimed at improving health, were giving away £2000 grants. 'Do you have an idea to help improve the health of your community?' I said to myself 'Yes, I do.' I had an idea of setting up a film and theatre production company dealing with mental health issues. So I applied and was given a date for interview just six days after my book launch. The book launch increased my confidence and I gave a good interview. Consequently I was given the grant. That's the thing I notice: whatever you do, it feeds the next moment. Negativity breeds more negativity; positivity fuels more positivity.

Slowly the reviews for the book came trickling in, I was too frightened to read them but they were all great. Here is a sample:

"Raw, harrowing and compelling. This is a worthy addition to the new genre of mad memoirs."- **Robert Dellar, Mad Pride**

"The frankness and ironic humour kept me turning the pages. This is the book I'll give to people who want to know what madness is really like."– **Liz Main, Mental Health Today**

"Thought-provoking, stark, brutal and exhilarating"– **Anne Mathie, Mind Out**

"An outstanding memoir about surviving childhood abuse and severe mental illness." - **Mind**

"Dolly's powerful and moving memoir tells her terribly difficult story in an astonishingly frank and honest way which, don't ask me how, somehow manages a streak of irony and dare I say it, even humour. It is an incredibly honest and determined account to record her personal struggle with mental illness." - **Barry Watts, Mind.**

"Dolly's memoir is a work of genius. Step aside Germaine Greer! Dolly's book and subsequent work in the film industry is providing real empowerment for women kind."- **Jason Pegler, founder of Chipmunkapublishing**

"In all its rawness and humour, it is a vivid account. This book is a valuable contribution to the body of literature that has been written by Survivors of the psychiatric system." **LTTV**

"I defy anyone to read this book and not be moved."
Ben Watson, Metamute

"This book is fabulous. She has created something I have never seen before." **Rosemary Moore, Mental Magazine**

"It is a book about hope and will be an inspiration to mental health survivors who read it." **Cath Collins, Lambeth Mind**

Not only did people think it was a well-written book, but was already beginning to help people. I was getting letters through Chipmunka from survivors and mental health professionals saying how much it helped them. A mental health nurse called Tisa Graham said, "It hurts me to think we as professionals are unable to meet the needs of vulnerable people and sometimes add to the stress and fail to help. If the government cannot provide the resources and adequate care, I believes it needs to come from 'below'. Thanks, Dolly, for giving me hope."

Another person said my book stopped her from committing suicide and gave her the courage to face her fears head on. It was so uplifting to get this response, that I could make people's souls feel lighter. The healing that kind of response had to my own emotional pain was colossal. This reflected my Buddhist practice, that happiness comes from helping others, and in the dissolving of the separation between humans.

Apart from the grant, The King's Fund, offered Leadership training. When I saw that, I thought, oh no,

I'm no leader. The other people on the course will be University graduates, or articulate professionals, and I will feel inadequate. But I really wanted the grant to set up my project so I said to myself I will grit my teeth and do it. The course was going to begin on January 2003.

In the meantime until then, I went to mental health groups to promote my book. One of them was the Critical Psychiatry meetings at Great Russell Street. There I met 'Listen To The Voices', an organisation, who at that time was using film to challenge ideas about the nature of 'mental illness'. In their bumph they say 'They wish to draw attention to the fact that when an individual is diagnosed as 'mentally ill' they often encounter socially exclusive practices and discrimination. LTTV believes that such a situation is more damaging and distressing to the individual than any mental health difficulties they may already have to cope with. The impact of a psychiatric diagnosis is far more reaching that just having contact with mental health services.' I thought, right on! At the meeting they were showing their work-in-progress, a film about the Draft Mental Health Bill.

LTTV also ran film and media training for survivors, so I contacted them to learn more about film-making. I ended helping on the film about the Bill, mostly doing camera work. The more I worked on the film, the more I realised The Mental Health Bill is a horrendous thing. Please, please explain something to me – where is the CARE in mental health care? Every person who has been through the system will tell their horror stories of how badly they were treated, of stripped searches, ECT, forced injections, indifferent nursing, etc, so a review of the mental health bill could have been an opportunity to improve this, but what do they use it for – more compulsory treatment, more horror for vulnerable people, more reason to distrust the system. This new legislature conflicts with Human Rights. How could that possibly be justified? If you were newly experiencing mental distress or having strange mental experiences, would you want to enter a system that could force treatment in your own home? No room for love, respect or trust? You're going to stay the fuck away, and become more unwell, more isolated, more alienated. You're going realise you're living in the 21st century and that psychiatry is still medieval, and that the majority of its practitioners are just drug pushers for the pharmaceutical companies. What you need is hope, but that can't be offered without side effects, it can't be offered with mental health professionals exchanging their role of carer for jailer.

Also explain this to me: that the majority of mental health professionals realise this mental health bill is unworkable and backward-sliding, that most mental health charities are against it, as are lawyers, carers and service users. So why is it still going through?

There was a Scrutiny Committee set up to look at this Bill, and they made over 100 recommendations to emphasise the rights, care and treatment of vulnerable people without the need for compulsion, but most of it was ignored.

The government seems to be taking its consultation for this Bill from inaccurate, nasty Tabloid reportage. This Bill feeds people's misconceptions on mental health issues. Doesn't matter that murder committed by a mentally ill person is minute, and that you are more likely to be killed a drunk 9-5er. To me, this bill is based on prejudice – nothing more. Care for vulnerable people seems very secondary.

When Creative Routes, the mad performance company I belong to, performed on the Liberty stage at Trafalgar Square, the Bill was represented as Fear Embodied. This Bill is a monster.

Any warmth the mental health system had is draining away to be as cold as a corpse, as welcoming as a handshake full of razor blades. This Bill won't decrease murders but increase them. I see the extra suicides by mad people, a hidden holocaust. But dead mad people are good for society, we're the empty-eaters, burden to the tax payers (!) I am fucking angry about this. But give me your worst and I will give you my best. No, I won't have an axe in my hand. Instead "I will not cease from mental fight nor shall my art sleep in my hand."

The only compulsory treatment orders there should be is this: That all service users have respect from all the professionals they deal with; that every service user has, if it is needed, good housing support and provision; psychological therapies to all who want it; social support and leisure activities and employment opportunities. That is the kind of treatment that should be compulsory. A treatment order that is solely based on coercion and forced drugging makes it look like they are punishment squads for people who dare to be different from the norm. I know there are some 'mad' people who are violent. But there are sane people who are violent, but not every violent person has medication forced on them.

I featured on both sides of the camera in LTTV's film DRAFT BILL. Apart from being a camera operator, I was interviewed at the Mad Chicks Event about it. Simon Barnett, one of the founders of Mad Pride and a man I hugely respect, was also interviewed at the Mad Chicks event, and what he said about it was spot on: "There's a famous poem, well, the truth of the poem was that first they came for the mentally ill, then they came for the learning disabled, and so on. If we allow the Bill to be passed, that is what sort of society we will be dealing with." The poem he talks about is Nazi Germany and how it dealt with its undesirables. They didn't go to the gas chambers overnight, but it began just like this Bill and built up from there. Us mad people are the litmus test for any kind of laws that deal with compulsion and social control, and it doesn't usually stop with us...

During the time the Nazis were in power, over 70, 000 mentally ill and learning disabled people were killed in psychiatric hospitals and 'killing centres'. The killing of other groups came next. This genocide was not committed by the SS but by nurses and doctors. A euthanasia program was developed by an organisation called Aktion T-4. It is horrific to read how nurses coaxed patients to drink the poison that would kill them. They did it in a compassionate tone. "Come on, it's good for you..."

Between 1939 and 1945 around about 200.000 disabled people were murdered by the Nazis. I am not saying that the Blair government are outright Nazis but more of a pastel shade of fascism. What else could you call the new mental health bill which is about the vicious eroding of human rights that it entails? And if you don't think refusing or downscaling life-saving heart treatment of another misunderstood group – people with learning difficulties – isn't a form of eugenics, then what is?

My passion for the cause was stirred.

Anyway, I loved film making, and it whetted my appetite for more. At my local library there were postcards advertising a TV and video production course at a place called the Community Zone in Streatham. I applied and was offered a place. Things were starting to come together.

The Community Zone is a media resource centre in an unassuming grey building on Palace Road in Streatham, right next to a huge estate, but stepping into the building was like stepping into a new world of colour, life and the magic of people who have passion. It was started by a wonderful woman called Karen Francis, feisty and determined to make the local community a better place and empowering people through education and training in things people actually wanted. To get training in film and other media areas is incredibly expensive. If you live in poverty it is hard to dream because most dreams come with a price tag attached, but people like Karen make so many dreams come true. The workshops I did at the Community Zone were the first positive learning experience I had. It was a learning experience with heart and soul – my kinda thing. Our teacher was a wonderful man called Alaistair Pirrie who used to be on Razzamatazz, and had many years experience in TV and radio as writer, director and producer. His teaching was not a sedate, academic practice. He told us stories of his time in the media to illustrate points and threw us into the deep end several times. I remember coming in one Saturday for class and Alastair say to me, "Dolly, you're gonna hit the ground running. I want to you write a script for a short drama from scratch during this lesson." "Wha?" was my stunned reply. "You can do it, Dolly, this is what it is like in the film business, full of pressure like this on a daily basis."

What could I do but go away and write? An hour later I came back with a script called 'Old Man', which was a dialogue between a father and daughter on a park bench without them knowing they were related to each other. The ambivalent feelings I had for my own father was inspiration for the script. The script was eventually made as an interconnecting film that held several other short films together. It worked really well and I was proud that my characters were moving outside my head into the real world, so to speak. At the Community Zone, I helped make a few other short films. I had a natural talent for camera work which first showed itself in my work with LTTV. Some of the other films I worked on was a 'Drum & Bass' short, and a piece on estranged fathers.

While that was still going on I began the Leadership Course with the King's Fund. It turned out to be really useful, in that how to handle people and get the most out of them. I was worried before the course started about the other people on the course being better than me. They were actually a lovely bunch and committed to their projects. We were all supportive of each other and it became a wonderful bonding experience.

It taught me that leadership is not imposing your will on others but to get the best out of people by inspiring them and respecting them, by providing opportunities and empowerment. The course taught me how to develop personal authority. Leadership is not telling people what to do; it is confidence, clear-headedness, approachability, making everyone feel important. Having personal authority is doing, despite the barriers involved, sometimes going against the grain rather than be part of the machine. My confidence flowered on this course. It gave me the practical tools to start up my own film and theatre production company called Mindfull Productions. I started off by providing drama workshops at the mental health centre in Brixton for people with severe mental health issues. We had a lot of fun with those. Watch the light of creativity eclipse the dark night of the soul, I told people. Artard said an amazing thing:

"Theatre is the double of life... Theatre is a revolt against the cosmos." Creativity for me was not only a personal expression but a way to connect with the universe and to light its dark corners and to protest any injustices.

There was art and creativity before there was even language. Life is a stage. Is life a show worth watching? What would make the show better? Can we change the ending? I think we can. Each one of us can create art *and* life.

Role is a social entity. When we meet people, we play different roles. You act differently when you're with your family than when you are with your friends. How do you ACT when you are with a mental health professional? Is he/she the director, making you act in the production called 'SANITY? Do you have control over the roles you perform? Life is a production you can be mindful of, something that you can create or perform in any way.

I also made films. The biggest film project I did was based on a man called William Collins who spent 36 years in Broadmoor.

I had attended a couple of the Critical Psychiatry meetings in London. There I introduced myself to quite a few people, one of them being Sara Stanton of LTTV. I also saw Rosemary Moore there; she was wearing a t-shirt advertising her website: www.mentalmagazine.co.uk. I sent her a review copy of 'Laughter' and she really liked it. She bought two more copies and asked me to send them to Janet Cresswell who was at Broadmoor Hospital and to Bill Collins who had just come out of the Broadmoor experience. He was in a low-secure forensic unit in Lambeth. As I lived locally I decided to give him his book personally. I phoned him and made a time to meet up in a café in Clapham. He was very shy and because he has been out of circulation so long, he was socially awkward. He told me a little of his story. He had attacked his ex-girlfriend and stabbed her. He gave himself up to police and was convicted of aggravated assault and sentenced to four years.

Some time into his jail sentence, he became very distressed about what he did to his ex-girlfriend and became unmanageable, so he was transferred to Broadmoor without a further trial. If he had stayed in jail, he would have been out in the early 60s, as it happens he was not released until the early 2000s.

This happens because special hospitals don't work to sentences. They only let you out when they feel like it. They don't even work to a criterion of mental health. It is a system of control rather than treatment, containment not care. Bill told me in bad old days, beatings by 'nurses'. He had his arm broken in two places by nurses in 1968. He also witnessed the racist murder of Michael Martin by nurses. Bill bravely offered to give evidence to the coroner regarding Michael Martin's death, but this offer was turned down.

Now out, he was nearly 60 and wanted to get a job. I thought his age and his history would make it extremely difficult to find one. In the end, he could only find a voluntary job at the Brunel Museum in Rotherhithe, which he excels at because it reflects his interest in engineering and science. One of the reasons he was in Broadmoor for so long was because he was 'treated' for schizophrenia when it was arguably the wrong diagnosis. It was finally decided he has Asperger's Syndrome, a milder form of autism, where there are social skills difficulties. There is nothing wrong with people with Asperger's, it just makes them slightly different, a difference you can detect in social situations, they don't always understand what socially appropriate behaviour is. Things are very much black and white for them. Subtlety is a challenge to them.

When I first met him he was at the Ward in the Community, situated as an annexe to Lambeth Hospital on Landor Road. It was supposed to be an introduction to the community when patients have their own flats. But that was just a hollow gesture. Ward in the Community was just another hospital setting, governed by power imbalances prevalent in psychiatry. It just had a nicer décor.

The staffing at the unit was abysmally bad. There were staff there that were ok and actually cared about the 'clients' there, but most were nauseatingly rude and nasty. I had a few kiss there teeth at me, insinuate that I am having an illicit relationship with Bill. (Of course, that I can be just a friend to someone that is male and much older than me goes way over their small minds). Yes, sometimes Bill can be difficult (he is only human after all, oh, I forgot, being human is anathema to psychiatry) but the psychiatry surrounding him is even more difficult and a sure way to drive him crazy by treating him like a child. You should watch a psychiatric nurse chide a 62 man to see why the mental health system is indecent and self-defeating.

The concept of freedom was obviously playing on my mind. I became a member of Human Writes, a charity that organises penpals for people on Death Row in the USA. I wanted to understand what the death penalty was like in reality. What I learned it is unfair, racist and that there are too many people on Death Row who are proved to be innocent. It is not a deterrent. Every place that has introduced the death penalty has had their murder rate go up not down. It is a tricky subject. If I lost my niece to a murderer, for example, I would want that bastard dead; it is an emotive subject. My main problem with the Death Penalty is that 'punishment' has become a business. I can just imagine companies who run privatised correctional facilities having brochures stating we can kill for less money. That I find obscene.

Because I am also a Buddhist, I wanted to put my compassion into action. I did become friends with my penpal Imara and made plans to visit him at San Quentin, just outside of San Francisco.

This was my second trip to the USA. The first one changed my life so I have affection for the place. But my second trip was not really as a tourist and America had decided to invade Iraq. So I was no longer wide-eyed. A lot of first experiences had by now become 6th, 7th, 8th experiences and not really fresh and invigorating. Or so I thought. But like everything I found, it just depends on the way you look at it. The odd depressive thought or series of thoughts would lurk and seek the negativity in everything I did. I thought: aw, travelling is just fatigue, jet lag, loneliness, touts trying to rip you off, and sore arses from sitting on planes, buses, etc. But there are always chances, apertures of light and guidance, if you keep your eyes open. I have come to believe nothing is an accident. Someone gave me a book, The Alchemist by Paulo Coelho. It is about a traveller in search of worldly treasure but finds spiritual treasure instead. In the book as he travels he gets robbed. He could have given up and gone home, and lost so much in the process. The following lines from the book stuck in my head and in an instant my perception flipped: 'As he mused about these things, he realised that he had to choose between thinking of himself as the poor victim of a thief and as an adventurer in quest of his treasure. "I'm an adventurer, looking for treasure," he said to himself.

After that I became an adventurer looking for treasure. What kind of treasure would I find in a country that was dropping bombs in a faraway land? Well, San Francisco is famous for its gold and the search for it.

In readiness for my trip I was listening to the song that has a line, "If you're going to San Francisco, make sure you have flowers in your hair." This was the soundtrack playing around me as I saw pictures in newspapers of an Iraqi man crying over the bomb-burnt corpse of his child.

The war in Iraq had just started. Stop signs in San Francisco had WAR graffittied under the word 'STOP', so STOP WAR signs were everywhere. Or signs with 'NO' then became 'NO WAR'.

But the people of San Francisco didn't let me down. I didn't meet one person over there for the war. In fact, I arrived in the city just after demonstrations where hundreds of people were arrested for demonstrating a freedom that the government said they were fighting in Iraq for.

I stayed at The Hotel Virginia, which was now an international youth hostel. My room had a bunk bed in it. I slept on the bottom bunk, and let any ghosts of the hotel take the top bunk. On the wooden underside of the top bunk were a lot of 'I was here' pen scrawls from travellers all over the world, quite a few from the UK: 'T&T were here', 'Two starving paddies were here!' 'Emma and Helen SF road trip' and 'Just checked my bank account on the net. Oh fuck, I'm broke again!'

On the room door was an earthquake warning poster 'DUCK – COVER – HOLD' it said. I remembered this

28

piece of advice and was quite disappointed that I didn't get a chance to try it out!

I took a cruise tour from Pier 39 and circled Alcatraz. There I passed some seals, one of which looked like Bobby, one of my dogs, and I missed all my dogs instantly in that moment. Back on dry land, I met a drag queen wearing fluorescent pink under an umbrella, grooving on a bench to some music with a plastic pink flamingo. She cheered me up.

I went to the tourist office near Market Street where Jack Kerouac once walked and had visions as described in 'On The Road'. Market Street was pretty cool in itself. I don't mean the shopping centre, but the guys wearing boards proclaiming that we were all going to hell, and the homeless people playing chess on the street with stockbrokers. At the tourist office the people before me in the queue were asking which was the best place to eat, best place to stay, and all that. When it was my turn, I kinda floored the guy behind the desk by asking for directions to San Quentin Prison. He was helpful anyway, whipping out a map and plotting my course with his chewed up biro.

It took two buses to get to the prison. One from the city to San Rafeal bus station, then one to the prison. The Bus station was a quintessential American bus stop with a small coffee shop. The nomad in me appraised it for mood and sustenance. There were beautiful hills and greenery in the background. There were toilets, a coffee shop, discarded newspapers and the resident drunk. What more could you want? It was a beautiful feeling, to be a traveller.

The bus driver was kind enough to tell me where the stop was for the prison, and the bus stop to take me back to San Rafael. It was much less a bus stop but an intersection on a country road.

Getting into the prison was not too bad actually. We were told to put our belongings in a locker, and then we had to wait on wooden benches in the waiting room. There were a lot of young Mexican women with their kids waiting with me. The pain in their young faces haunted me. Do people realise how expressive their faces are, their words saying one thing and their eyes another?

In the processing area, I had to take my jacket and shoes off and put it through an x-ray machine, and then I had to go through the machine myself. Out through the door I was in the sunlight again and met with another prison officer who stamped the back of my hand with an ultra-violet Disney Character. Disney character? Was I going into Disneyland? I guess they use cartoon characters so as to not frighten the kids that get their hands stamped, but nevertheless it was very bizarre, entering a Disneyworld that kills people.

There was a waiting area before we were taken into a cage to conduct our visit. It was seedy and grim and only slightly more accommodating than the wired visiting cages housed there. There were a couple of vending machines where we could buy snacks for our condemned friends and family. I was waiting with an elderly white woman visiting her son and a young Mexican woman and her child visiting her husband. It was a quite bizarre situation in that we were chitchatting a stone's throw away from a place that executes people, people who we know.

I entered the visiting cage with some snacks and a couple of can of cold drinks and waited quite a while. It turned out the times got mixed up and Imara had been waiting for me earlier and now he was asleep. While I waited, I looked around the cell. There was nothing but two plastic chairs and a plastic bin with a transparent plastic bag. To the left of me was a Black guy and a Black woman; to my right was a middle-aged white guy – he looked like a redneck – with an elderly woman, I guess his mother. She bought him loads of stuff to eat and he was munching away asking about family.

These visiting cages were arranged in two rows, so there was another row in front of me. In one these cages was a tattooed Mexican guy with his mom, dad, wife and kid. The kid was happily playing with his father. Poor kid. His father may have committed a terrible crime but the kid didn't, but he was going to be punished also. The country he will pledge allegiance to in school will kill his father. Somehow I don't think the kid will grow up easily.

Finally Imara was brought outside the cage. He smiled shyly at me, I smiled back. They un-handcuffed him and he sat opposite me. "So we finally meet," I laughed. We didn't know what to say to each other for a little while. I offered him snacks and a cold drink. He didn't touch the snacks but really savoured the cold drink. I could tell he hadn't had a canned drink for a while.

Imara told me there was a man who has been on the row for years, who doesn't talk to anybody except the small people he sees on the palm of his hand. The conditions of death row have made madness for this man the only place to be. He had lost his mind, and they were going to kill him too. Officially there are no mentally ill people on death row because it is illegal to execute a mentally ill person. But the reality is there is a high percentage of mentally ill people waiting to be killed by their country, most made mad by the hell of their environment. Most don't have adequate legal representation; some even had tax lawyers fighting for their lives.

Imara talked more on the 2nd visit. He told me there were guys on the row who had been there for over 20 years and still had their wits about them. They used the time to educate themselves. Imara learned from one in particular, Adisa, who was one of the co-writers to 'AFTERLIFE'. Adisa told Imara that the system in America who intrinsically racist and the Black person will always be at the bottom. This made Imara angry and he said, 'Let's fight the system. Let's start a revolution!" Adisa shook his head in the negative and said, "No, revolutionise this." He said, pointing to his temple.

San Quentin is situated in a beautiful area near a quiet bay. It was a very well-off neighbourhood. After my first visit, I went to a secluded beach to contemplate my visit. I was there about an hour and only saw one person, a local walking his dog. We chatted for a bit and I told him I missed my dogs in London. He then said, "Did you visit someone at the prison?" "Yeah, a friend on death row." "Yeah, I figured you were a death row visitor. They always come to the beach to think, I think maybe the sea is a calming influence."

The power of the feeling that I was allowed to leave Death Row sent shivers through me. The ride back to the city I was thinking, 'Freedom! Freedom!" Somehow it didn't feel like an American thing.

Back in the UK, I spent the spring and summer initiating Mindfull Production projects, like filming Bill Collins and his struggle to free himself from the mental health system; I ran drama workshops in Brixton and Oval House Theatre, and instigated a collective poem on the theme of madness. Over 30 poets took part and created a startling piece of literature. See for yourselves.

This is Madness
As you know I breathe and smile and fall into velvet trances,
glazed with love and hopelessly charred with disapproval
No other action left save my removal.
touched only by the ECT stigma of this alienation
I breathe and smile and fall, I fall as you well know
Too well this florid reverie this madness
but say my love remind me have I taken my pill?
as I can only see the world through touch and feel
I, beast. Over you, in you, through you, I beast you.
Do I not have beauty? The way you look at me, I think not.
In such a song I -am/will be- the undying loser, giver of
Unsatiable desires under the penstroke of doctors nimble fingers
We are the straw people. We are the hollow people –

leaning together
Now is a little time of the past, mixed with a little time of the
Future with nothing in the middle, travelling at the speed of light
This poet saw a magpie within a dream within a dream and the poet knew that the world was mad
The poet couldn't sleep because a nightmare woke him up. In the dream he was driving all night. Lost control of the wheel, not knowing when he was going to crash.
Not caring and not cared for, courting death
As only people, drowned in their mortal fear of emotional expression,
afraid to externalise their dreams, can do.
Man man, woman woman, we're all the same until that moment the pressure drops, madness descends and sits on our shoulders waiting to see who will claim it today
as we hold our breath and count to seventeen eighteen, seventeen eighteen
Never getting beyond, keep returning keep returning keep returning keep returning keep returning if this record ever stops I will fall out I will eat all, burning
With none to walk down this soapy work... If I had more dirt I could float time but who wants feet marked with the smoke of this flowerbed?
100 02 1000, or just forever, off into the netherland it asks you to know yourself and it never whispers in a naked purple haze, the body burns
To the gentle whistling of the flute that transgresses certain boundaries,
Unaware of its subtle power behind the flame
I promise you signs -- dust, oceanic tragedies, stars that look like eagles

Curled talons in the sky, wrapped round my mind
scratching me out till I write in lines
earthquakes, blood moons, an everlasting eclipse
I promise you Nature's rage - as it exists - within me
RARRR!!! As fruit: rind, stoned, mashed by madness. I combine
an electronic insanity with an enlightened mind.
And a grief that does not look like a heaven that has betrayed us
Squeezed between two white walls I explode in a wake up call
Fall as a nano jump in an elevator pit
I swirl around in the blender which is now my life
Whirling, swirling, cut up, enlightened but still controlled by strife
The rage exists, then exits, bringing calm and serenity
Giving birth to nature's beauty once more
Does the cycle begin again, the reincarnation, the whirling of the
Start and rise of this madness once again?
I pick and eat shiny fruits off the trees I can still find left standing
And grow strong with the effort of love
Yet, I struggle to disentangle the myriad noises emanating from the universe,
As they merge into a powerful mantra that shatters my powerful self
I'm alone in my bedroom, paranoid, scared, sweaty, clammy.
The ghosts in the hall outside bang their fists on my door
And I try to pretend everything is normal
But bleached by insanity, I lean against the white wall,
Lost within the crumbling brickwork, losing hold
The whisper shouts the sense out, away from my

grasp
As of tomorrow this world starts spinning
My way? Against you – and your everything
Lick me quick for I am silver, the taste of thinking freed
My am is chained, but willingly, my love is growing
seed
When you see me coming, when you touch my roar
Then you know I was serious the whole damn time
Mechanical spiked judgments cattleprod and shock me
into a tight closed ball of submission: until the whiff of
lavender in the garden I planted seeps through: until I
unfurl a finger to stroke the minute complex silk of my
dog's warmly proffered head: until an oceanic skyblue
peace the widest heart of everyone opens up down my
body oh world without end where none of us has ever
failed to abide
I'm a headless person with no body
I'm a headless person with nobody
Reach out and touch me
Or accept this is madness
That this is madness.

I got really into poetry. The Beat Poets had always
inspired me and I wanted to be like them. I wanted to
perform my stuff too, but didn't want to go through the
academic route. I found most of British poetry
published by major publishers a bunch of middle-class
tripe who didn't understand real pain, and if they did
you didn't see it in their poetry. It was tepid, polite
agony. I hunted poetry that would tear your skin off
and leave you exposed, or provide protection if you
were already skinless. So I scoured the internet for
poets like me. I found a website called Litkicks based
in the US. I introduced myself on their forum and

asked for useful contacts. Somebody gave me Barry Fitton's email details. I emailed him and gave him my story. He told me he was arranging an international poetry festival in August in Amsterdam and invited me to perform. I jumped at the chance. It felt great that my poetry performing debut would be at an international poetry festival in a foreign country. He also had a radio show on the internet and invited me to participate in that too.

Barry Fitton is quite a remarkable person, and an unconventional character. He left school at fifteen and worked in a factory for a little while. He realised, like me, that you are not born to work in a factory for shitty wages, but to see the beauty and poetry of life, and point out where the world is going wrong. Most of civilized humanity is in huge denial about what life is really about. Barry understands this and he absolutely screams his poetry to a world that doesn't want to listen. His motto is: 'Have poems, will travel' and he has done the overland route to India, Greece and Ibiza. He also has done things like run a cat rescue and lived in squats. A man with a big heart to go along with his big mouth.

I booked my ticket and flew over. Barry gave me instructions on how to reach The Kirk, a derelict Catholic Church that was now a squat and arts centre. I found my way there easily.

The Kirk was a deserted catholic church on a corner of a street lined with shops and supermarkets - a towering presence. On the notice board out front instead of advertising services and absolutions and the opportunity to confess there were posters for the squatter meets, poetry readings, and anarchy demonstrations. It also had its fair share of graffiti. The one I remember is SAVE THE KIRK. Its current residents were battling the authorities who wanted to demolish it to put up a supermarket. It didn't matter there were 2 supermarkets less than 100 metres away. Barry suggested the church was best served as a community arts centre and was therefore of much more benefit than a 3rd supermarket on the road. The city disagreed and they eventually knocked it down. Art always loses out. Artists are too poor to give the decision makers backhanders.

Inside it was as dusty as an old church and endless progression of congregations – both religious and secular – could give to the air – dead skin lasting longer than any good intention of its owners. Ask the dust anything.

As I entered the church the first thing I saw was the stained glass. A mute light was shining through them, casting beautiful hues on emptiness. Some of the glass was broken. There were no pews, but a ragged collection of chairs and scruffy sofas salvaged from skips. It was a strong visual image, creating a memory that would elicit a calm happiness.

Barry was rushing about, getting everything ready for the event, but he stopped in his tracks to welcome me and make me feel more at home. He showed me to my bed, which was a tatty sofa. I knew it would be crawling with dust mites but I didn't care. After I had a short nap on it, I went back downstairs to the main church to help out, mainly with clearing up and in the kitchen.

The walls of the main church were lined with strange junk (such as a doll's head in a jar of vinegar) and paintings of the artists who used the church as a studio. I spent an hour watching two painters working on their pieces. One of them knew I was watching him and he gave me a good show, by not standing directly in front of his painting and giving me a fair showing of smiles and ass. There was one painter there, a Spanish guy moping because he couldn't sell his paintings, and washed his art in the wrong kind of spirits. Whilst I was there he sold one painting. He dashed out and came back with a bag full of beers. His masterpiece deferred for what reason, I don't know. We artists are a sensitive bunch. But not as sensitive as street cleaners with higher IQs than doctors, as one report found there is such a thing.

There were a bunch of Spanish anarchists there who did nothing but smoke dope on ragged sofas and eat all the food of others. I thought, these kids have a fucked up understanding of anarchy. Most of the other residents of the church were anarchists as I was, but that meant fair share of everything, including work and food. Barry would shake his head every time he passed the group. On the night of the reading he told them off for chucking litter and cigarette butts on a floor that had just been cleaned. There was always music playing in the background, punk, jazz, classical, blues and Jimi Hendrix.

There was nothing left for me to do at the church until the radio show that night so I walked around the city in broken shoes. I'm one of those people who wear clothes and shoes until they have fallen apart. I get especially attached to my shoes and do feel sad when I have to get rid of them. Eventually it was evening and I was heading back to the Kirk. About to cross the road towards the church, I heard Barry call my name. He was sitting at a pavement café nearby, eating pizza. He had finally got the poetry reading program together and it was looking pretty good. He introduced me to a poet from Liverpool called Roger Cliffe-Thompson, a protégé of the great Liverpool poet Jim Bennett. I spent a lot of the next few days with him; he was a great one for anecdotes about the poetry scene. One my favourite stories of his is about this old lady who looked very prim and proper with her hair in a bun who got on the stage and said something like: "If life is treating you badly, all you have to do is this." And she gave life – and the audience- the two-fingered swear sign. What a cool woman. Both Roger and I had a soft spot of for that crazy Barry. Roger told me when Barry stayed at his house in Liverpool Barry didn't close the windows of his room because he thought it would disturb the pottery on the window sills. His compassion and kindness is palpable. Roger went back to the church, whilst Barry and I headed for the radio station.

Our stop before the radio station was some relaxation at a pavement café, drinking beers and coffee and hot chocolate. It felt good and right and magical. Barry ordered a special kind of coffee – can't remember the name – the Dutch waiters couldn't understand his Rochdale accent. He was telling anecdotes of the poetry reading: one time he coaxed a shy performer to get on stage to do his kinetic art, but once there someone in the audience was screaming like a banshee, putting the poor fella off. Barry demonstrated the scream to the horror of some of the patrons of the café. We were too weird for even Amsterdam's laid back residents. I loved that Barry. As the evening wore on, more of Barry friends and confederates joined us and crowded around the table. Jennifer Arcuni, an American poet living and working in Amsterdam, asked me how I liked Amsterdam. I told her I loved it. "You might be like me and not be able to leave." Then I met my first bluesman, T-bone Fisher, and he didn't disappoint the perception I had of them as cool. Raspy-voiced, red-eyed, taciturn, drinking, smoking, projecting a rawness and a coolness that he needed for his music. Then I saw a man talking to his bicycle. The Dutch love their bicycles. Then another bluesman turned up, a harmonica player who spoke more into his mobile phone than to us. He was also a promoter and was haggling with someone in Belgium. Barry asked him to tell me the story of his time on a psychiatric ward. "Yeah, I was sleeping. When I work up, my shoes were gone. The police found me walking about with no shoes and took me to the local mental ward. I tried to tell them I was a well-known blues harmonica player, that I played with B. B. King. And they were like, of course, you are, like they didn't believe me. So I had to spend the weekend on the ward. I couldn't see the doctor till Monday. When I saw the doc, I told him to please look at my website to see I was who I actually was, and he did and so set me free... without any shoes."

Barry invited him to play on his radio show, but he begged off and wandered down the street, trying to contact someone on his mobile. We were waiting for the radio show technician, the male-to-female-and-back to male again transsexual. I kind of had an idea of a transvestite shimmying down

41

the road in a sequined dress, so was disappointed to see a long-haired young lad in a t-shirt and jeans with his bicycle. He sat with us at the café but was anxious to get started with the programme.

He took us to a doorway in building that lead up to stairs and more stairs. The actual radio station was in a loft-like area, where the only access to it was a ladder that looked like it belonged to a bunk bed. It was a dingy little set-up, dusty and badly decorated, with underground party posters hanging limply from a wall with begrimed cello tape. All the equipment was stacked into cramped corners and were dusted with cigarette and spliff ash.

There was just the one microphone on a table for the guest speakers so we sat at the table and took turns on the hot seat and kept banging knees on the table legs when we swapped positions, so our first words on the radio programmes were 'shit' and 'fuck'. Barry was hilarious in that he kept looking at the radio man's small tits. Obviously whatever hormone he was taking wasn't totally out of his system. The small-titted radio technician warned us that the air extractor had to be switched off while we were on air otherwise there would be too much interference. But Barry was smoking so much weed, the place was too fogged and crazed, so we had to keep it on for the most part and quickly switch off when on air. Because Barry was so stoned he would keep motioning at me to switch it on when we were on the air, and switch it off when we were off air. I didn't know what I was doing any more but enjoyed doing it nonetheless.

I read some of my poems. T'bone played some Blues, and Jennifer read some of her stuff. Barry sat in his seat, very stoned with a silly smile on his face. At least he stopped looking at the radio man's tits.

I crawled into bed back at the squat in the early hours of the morning to the sound of rats scuttling in the attic.

The next morning I explored the city and searched for some furry clogs for a friend. I couldn't believe that it took me hours to find furry clogs. It was like searching for the Holy Grail that is nice to touch and tickles your nose when you try to smell it to see if somebody else has worn them.

When I got back to the squat, it was early afternoon and the Norfolk contingent had arrived, well, most of them. This was a group of Norwich poets that went under the name of The Poetry Cubicle. They had all piled into a tram. The trams in Amsterdam are very long and as they boarded the group got split up. Most of them got off at the right stop, but two of them missed their stop and didn't arrive at the church until the performance began in the evening. The poor things didn't even know the name of the church so it took them hours to find us.

I helped prepare for the gig. Barry wanted to screen a film he collaborated on. But we didn't know how to work the projector, not being very technical. Embarrassingly we discovered what the problem was – we had forgotten to switch the thing on. I was a bit disappointed the problem had been solved because that meant I had nothing really to distract me until the actual performance. I didn't want to think about performing until I actually had to do it.

The night kicked off with this weird poet called Julius Joker whose act comprised of jumping around and off things. I don't remember a word of his poetry and his madness was too forced, too artificial. A few other forgettable acts came on and then Roger from Liverpool came on. His poetry is fresh, funny, political and personal. One of his poems poked fun of the uniformity of youth's choice of clothing, called "I've Got a Tick on me Head" inspired by the tick logo of Nike. Roger has a strong Liverpudlian accent, and a lot of the Dutch couldn't understand him. One confused Dutch person said, "What, he's English!"

There were a few more poets before it was my turn. Barry became poetry avenger, making sure the audience was quiet enough to be receptive to the poetry.

My time to perform was coming nearer and nearer. How is it possible to perform without sitting on a toilet at the same time? I asked myself. My churning stomach was stealing the sound of my voice, the weight of my inflection. Would I perform the poetry of the catatonic, lips moving but poetry going awol. "I don't think I can do this," I said to Barry. "Of course you can," and he pushed me onto the stage. I read from my book 'Eloquent Catatonia'. I was supposed to do a fifteen minute set but only did ten. I wanted to get off the stage as soon as possible. But once I got off, I wanted to get back on again. Something had been triggered in me, I was getting the early symptoms of the performing bug. I had that slightly feverish high that my bones were made of bubbles. When I flew home to England, I am sure the plane flew just a bit higher because I was in it.

Less than a week after my poetry debut in Amsterdam, I was invited to perform at the Mad Pride gig at The Garage in North London. At my book launch, the people who stood out for me were the people from Mad Pride. Their spark, their zest and kindness made an impression on me.

It was the book launch of Ted Curtis, a quiet guy into his penguins. He has a website stating that 'a revolution without penguins is already lost', and I agree with him. He is very funny, sardonic guy, always coming up with these amazing one-liners. 'By Theft and Murder' details his experiences in Palestine with the organisation ISM (International Solidarity Movement). It really is a great book that opened my eyes for the first time to the day-to-day hell the Palestinians endure. Ted went over there to take part in non-violent direct action against the Israeli occupation. He read from his book to kick off the night.

Also sharing the stage was the comedian Jeremy Hardy who also went over to Palestine. Hugh Mulhall read from his book 'AKA A Memoir of The Divine Ms Thing', Ben Watson read from his 'Shitkicks and Doughballs' and I read from my book of poetry 'Maenad Angel Poetics'. I was shitting myself but enjoyed myself too. I loved everyone there, they were all uniquely beautiful, but my favourite person of the night was James Macdougall – described on the Mad Pride website as a rock star, comedy prophet, in-yer-face rebel, poser of awkward questions. He heckled for most of the night and tried to get his dick out of his trousers but was either too drunk or really not that motivated enough to carry out the deed. At the end of the gig, he finally got his floor spot. Bless.

But that and my time in Amsterdam was the beginning of my poetry reading career, since then I have performed at the Red Gate Poetry, the 291 Gallery, Brixton Art Gallery and many other places. The soul a balloon that finally had some air to it, so the rush, the high of performance was becoming addictive

Also I began my public speaking career, which when I was at my most shyest, and isolated, with a social phobia that turned people into pain, and eyes into razors, I would have never believed it if you told me that I would be on the stage and that people would listen attentively to my every word. It would have been inconceivable just a few months previously. Then I would have told myself, I couldn't do it. All it took were a few people like Jason Pegler and Barry Fitton to say, yes, you can do it, Dolly. It just took one thought in my head, "I *can* do it." And then I was able to do it. For every fear you face, you are just that little bit stronger because when a similar situation appears, you can't really say I can't do it because you have done it before, your insecurity becomes disingenuous, and you also remember the high of doing it and sense of achievement for doing so.

One of my earlier speaking engagements meant going up to Newcastle. I have lived in the UK all my life but I still hadn't visited most it of yet, so I was eager and excited to see my own country.

Invited by Launchpad, a user-led mental health organisation in Newscastle, who gave a great review of my book and made me a patron of their charity, I headed up there by train. I came up for their women's event. I had just come off a Buddhist retreat and was feeling cool and calm when I stepped off the train. I was met by Launchpad's 2 resident (male) philosophers who took me to the local pub and dysfunctioned me in a matter of minutes with their talk. One of the things discussed was penguins without arseholes!

I loved those guys but was glad when Miranda, another member of the organisation came to take over the hospitality. An evening with Miranda and her partner Keith de-stressed me nicely for the following day.

Before I was first hospitalized a psychiatrist said to me a stay in hospital would be an oasis of calm – it wasn't, far from it. But this woman's event entitled 'Blissful' was an oasis. Just what a stressed woman of the 21st century needed. It took the holistic approach to healing, living. It was also an opportunity to spoil yourself. There were Indian head massages, henna tattoos, reflexology, and drumming, among other things. I wanted to take part in the drumming session, but because I was preparing, I didn't have time to put my name down. I had to make do with drumming on my table. Still, I enjoyed myself. I was there to tell my story, a kind of condensed version of my book, and how writing your life story does so much for you. It was so cool to sign people's copies of the book and to hear that reading the book helped them. That's the best thing about it and makes me glad of writing a book that I had thought once maybe exposed too much.

I was given a table to talk around. The women who came to speak to me were amazing, I didn't want to only tell my story but hear theirs too. Instantly I saw a direct correlation between abuse and mental distress. I was angry that the best society could give some of these women to help them through their pain was a sedating drug that would make sure they wouldn't be much of a nuisance. Thumbs up to all those involved with 'Blissful' for showing there are other ways to heal. I told some women to either write their story or at least tell it. Their lives shouldn't be what they think are dirty secrets they have to hide. One woman shook her head sadly and said, "I can't, it's too painful. And besides, nobody wants to hear it." That's what I thought once. I now know that to be untrue. I said to some of the women who came to talk to me, with my book in my hand, "I can close the book on my painful past now." This may sound flippant but a strange thing happened when I first read my book after it was published. When your pain is inside you, along with your bad memories, it is easy to self-hate. But when I read my book, I felt an immense empathy for all the characters in my book, even for myself, and I had a better understanding and respect for my life. I went through shit, made a lot of mistakes, but I could see I was only human with the right to be happy, who could laugh and love.

At the beginning of the Blissful event, a couple of women spoke about their experiences with mental health services. One woman was given a small gift-wrapped box by, I think, a mental health professional, and was told something beautiful was inside it. She opened it to find a mirror. Low self-esteem and mirrors don't mix, but she was touched and began to believe maybe she was beautiful. Of course she was. Of course we all are. Every single woman who went to the event was beautiful.

One of the reasons for mental distress in women is the inability to believe they are beautiful. If you want to see a mad woman in pain, tell a woman who has been abused that she is beautiful, you will never see so much agony and distress in a human's eyes. My last book, filled with the pain and self-hate of my growing up, closed when I was beginning to discard the belief that I was ugly.

Out of the blue, I got a letter and postcard from a woman called Sarah Taylor, formerly of Southwark Arts Collective but now with a mental health arts group called Creative Routes. She had spoken to Sound Minds and they recommended me to her. The postcard she sent me was a quote from Kafka. It said: '*You do not need to leave your room, remain sitting at your table and listen. Do not even listen, simply wait, be quite still and solitary. The world will freely offer itself to you to be unmasked, it has no choice. It will roll in ecstasy at your feet.*' After reading those words, I knew I was going to like this woman. I contacted her and we met up and she invited me to take part in the performance company, who were doing workshops with the help of The Young Vic.

Our first big event was a show at the Young Vic in January 2004. We had our sights set high for Routes as an organisation, and had no idea we would go beyond our wildest expectations.

We started as a small group of about 30, a drumming group and a drama group. We had workshops in the cold aisles of St Peter's Church on the Walworth Road. Our aim was to put on a production at the Young Vic Theatre. Because a tree with roots was part of the logo of Creative Routes, a tree was going to be our centrepiece as idiosyncratic prop, metaphor and inspiration for the production. Our tree was made of ropes and bicycle wheels and Japanese umbrellas. Our performance comprised of drumming waking the poetry and the people out of the trees. There were eight performer/poets and I was one of them. My performance poem was called 'There are no doors'.

We played to a packed house. I found performing exhilarating. I got hooked on the acting bug, well and truly. I had the time of my life. I loved working with other mad, artistic people; I saw pure magic in them. Some people think those who live through mental health difficulties are weak, but all I saw was strength. For example, one of my fellow performers said she didn't want to get out of bed, could barely talk, but because she didn't want to let her fellow players down, she battled through her fatigue and fear to do the show.

I felt my life slowly fill my veins again, into something I liked wearing. No, loved wearing.

I was just so hungry for experiences and making up for lost time. I felt I had wasted my life; I wanted to squeeze the juice out of life and swallow the fire of stars. So anything that interested me I signed up for. I signed up for Disability Equality Training with SHAPE, the disability arts organisation. One day I stared at the huge white pile of my writings in my room, it was so mountainous, I think one night I found a Sherpa sleeping in there. I had books published and scripts filmed but not a play as of yet. So I dusted off the script 'Acts of Madness' and got to work on it. I applied for a grant from the Scarman Trust to put the play on and forgot about it for a while. I also searched for a theatre mentor in readiness and preparation for putting on my play.

I found a great mentor in Michael Walling, creative director of Border Crossing, an astounding theatre company specialising in world theatre and performance art. As its name suggests, its aim is to cross borders between cultures and artforms. I was so honoured to be able to learn a lot about theatre from them. I worked on a production called Bullie's House. It was the British première of Thomas Keneally's powerful and emotive play about Aboriginal Australia. It toured during the Spring, with a cast including Aboriginal actors. It was a remarkable educational experience. I learned about stage management and running a touring theatre company, and so much about Aboriginal culture. A couple of the actors, Natasha Wanganeen and Heath Bergersen, in the production were also in the beautiful Australian feature film Rabbit-Proof Fence, which also starred Kenneth Branagh. They stayed at my flat during their time in the UK. I had some strange looks from my neighbours because it is unusual to Aboriginal People in Streatham, South London. Especially with them didgeridooing in the garden. My role was as production assistant, and my various tasks were finding props, such as 1950s style bucket. Where am I going to find one of those, I asked myself. I guess somebody up there was looking after me, or at least keeping an eye out for discarded buckets, because the first thing I saw when I went to my local rubbish dump was a 1950s style bucket! I was also a script prompter during rehearsals, and spent a lot of my time distributing publicity material around London. I came along for some of the tour, like the Newbury Corn Exchange, and became a theatre roadie, which I loved. I don't know what the attraction is but my heart goes aflutter when the van doors swing open and we offload and set up. I continue to do this with Creative Routes, and our performance equipment has included an oversized electric plug, about a third of the size of a human. First in and last out, and I love it.

After decades of just sitting around and watching TV, I discovered I was a workaholic after all. When my stint with the Aboriginal play was done, I embarked on a few poetry gigs with Barry from Amsterdam, starting off with a Survivors Poetry gig at the Diorama in London, sharing the stage with the legendary Jean Binta Breeze. I was slowly honing my performance skills and steadily selling the poetry books I had self-published.

Survivors Poetry is a national literature and performance charity, set up in 1992 by four poets with first-hand experience of the mental health system. Simon Jenner, the director of Survivors Poetry, gave me a charming review of my poetry book 'Eloquent Catatonia'. He said: "She is a superb, contained performer and a curiously magical poet. This comic layering of real and surreal is something Sen is well-versed in. She has made an original and arresting debut." Kind words indeed.

I offered to publish Barry Fitton's life's work. It was an ambitious project, because rather than do the usual A5 without photos, we attempted an A4 book which included artwork and photos. I shipped it off to the printers in readiness to do a book tour with Barry. But things didn't quite go as planned. There was a postal strike in Oxford where the printers were, so we began the book tour without the ... book! One of our stops was the Poetry Cubicle in Norwich who were at the Amsterdam gig. We went up there and performed at a pub in a very strange village. If I was slightly bonkers at the time, I would think I had entered the village of the damned. We got caught up in a village scarecrow festival. There were scarecrows with shopping trolleys, there were scarecrows with fishing rods, there was an elaborate – and disturbing – display of a scarecrow being knocked down by a car. But the best scarecrow prize had to go to a scarecrow Barry spotted. He saw this man fixing up a scarecrow. As Barry took out his camera to take a picture, the man turned around and was the spitting image of the scarecrow! They were both wearing the same shirt, trousers and clothcap. If I were to recreate a doppelganger I wouldn't make it out of straw. That village was so creepy Dorothy and the real Scarecrow would have travelled around it on their way to the Wizard of Oz.

Well, seeing that the wicked witch of the east was doing her work in that village, I didn't think we would get a receptive audience. The audience we did have were the pub's locals, they were somewhat bemused. I had dreams later of performing in that pub and the whole audience was made of scarecrows. Jesus, that

Norwich trip had made a strong impression for the wrong reasons. But I had fun anyway.

Back in London, I began my disability awareness training course with SHAPE. It helped me understand the experience of disability clearer using the social model of disability, which in a nutshell maintains that disability is a socially manifested problem, that if environmental factors were addressed, such as accessible transport, there is no disability. For example, if a person of restricted growth had things adapted to their height, where is the disability? The only disability that remains is in the mind of the prejudiced. The medical model, which is the opposite of the social model, says that your disability is your problem, something that is broken that needs to be fixed, and that *you* have to fit into society.

For those of us who is mad, if we weren't forced to behave in the way society wants us to behave and think, half our pain would be diminished.

The social model is an influential tool for empowerment, but it needs legislative power behind it. To that end, the Disability Discrimination Act (DDA) came into full effect in 2005 and covers things like employment, provision of goods, facilities and services, education, and physical premises. Basically, the act means it is unlawful to offer less favourable treatment to disabled people.

One of the things we learned from the people who knew about it was that the DDA was pretty toothless, not enough bite to make an obvious dent in the disabling elements of society. There were enough loopholes in the Act to wriggle out of.

I remember one instance with Sarah and her enabling dog Gem. We had just attended the Mad For Arts launch at Tate Modern on Mental Health Day 2004. A bunch of us, including Creative Routers, and some media people from Mad For Arts, decided to have a drink at the nearby Founders Arms pub. Sarah was not allowed in because of her dog Gem. We pointed out that she was an enabling dog and that they were breaking the DDA. The manager, a nasty troll with a Hitler moustache and obvious dictatorial sensibilities, just smirked at us. He said the Health and Safety act had precedence over the DDA and on those grounds he could do what the fuck he wanted. He was an obvious misogynist because he was only aggressive to the woman, and I noticed he had a hard-on as he spat in our faces. I wanted to thump the bastard, forget road rage, I was developing disability rage. "You fucker!" I sneered at him as I left the pub. As we went outside ready to leave, a more sympathetic bar staff told us the Brewery sent every pub a list of how to wriggle out of the DDA. Isn't it awful that major companies don't see the Act as a chance to improve their services and take advantage of the £50 Billion annual spending power of disabled people but actually spend time and money trying to wriggle out of it? We did a mass walkout in protest. Most of the media staff stayed, their talk about fighting for equality was obvious hypocrisy.

I found out personally for myself what could have been an empowering act had very much the potential to be a disempowering one. My mum has been profoundly deaf since she was two. Her best friend Dawn is also profoundly deaf. They are inseparable; they go everywhere together. One of their favourite things to do is Bingo, and it is convenient that Streatham Hill Bingo is just a stone's throw from where my mum lives. Because of a variety of disabilities, which include deafness, arthritis and thrombosis, their choice of seating is limited. They found their place where both of them could view the screens with the numbers and where there was adequate legroom. The other Bingo regulars knew this was Mum's and Dawn's place and would look after it for them or explain to newcomers 'that's where 2 deaf women sit so they can see the screen', and successive managements informally confirmed this agreement. One day, they went there and found 2 other people in their seats. These weren't newcomers but well-known troublemakers. Dawn asked the assistant manager called Leroy but he wouldn't even speak to the two other women about Dawn's and Mum's deafness, because he was friends with them.

I went over to talk to this assistant manager and basically he told me to that there were plenty of other seats for my mum and Dawn to sit. I said to him they had access issues, he told me his mum has disabilities so he knew all about it, which is so unbelievingly patronising. Only my mum knows her access issues, and only I know mine – until we tell other people what they are. But it was pointless to do this here. He wasn't listening. His friends were going to sit where they liked, and my mum and her friend were denied access to a service. "I am going to get the DDA onto this," I told him. "Go ahead." He said. He knew it didn't have any teeth.

I rang the manager of the Bingo, Mandy, not long after, to put my mum's case across. I couldn't get a word in edgeways. She was so rude, I was left shaken. She later told the Disability Rights Commission that I was abusive and racist on the phone. I just have to bring that part of the situation up to people who know me or work with me and they get angry, because anyone who knows me knows I get passionate but never abusive and that the accusation that I am racist is utterly ridiculous. I am not White firstly - the Manager did not know this. Secondly, I have been under physical threat many a time because I have stood up to racists, and thirdly I was an active campaigner for rights of BME groups in the mental health system.

The Disability Rights Commission took up the case but dropped it soon after because Streatham Hill Bingo Hall said that they could provide witnesses – some of their workers - to my abuse and racism. We couldn't win. We were trying to fight bullshit with honesty, and bullshit has thousands of year's history of having the upper hand.

Fighting for equality, my arse. Lip service with a darker shade of Bullshit. Society seemed to have a vested interest in making me feel like shit. What had changed from a few years back, I no longer believed I was shit. I do get angry easily but it no longer slipped into the sphere of aggression and violence as it once did. I knew her karma would came back to haunt the manager. What a disgusting soul to have, you poor woman.

The year was not halfway over, and I had already packed into it a few years of experience. Some of it good, some of it not so good.

Creative Routes provided the unique opportunity to experience discrimination on an organisational level. One of the best examples was our experience with Tate Modern. Not only were the security guards behaviour overtly abusive to certain members of our group, the outreach worker said this did not happen, without any investigation, another case in point that our word is not taken seriously because we are survivors. Then the outreach worker refused to work with us unless we had a 'professional' go-between such as an occupational therapist, like she needed 'protection' from us or we were too stupid to relate to her on a professional level. Incidents like this infuriate me but it also inspires me to be stronger and more dedicated. I also had my fun by making a t-shirt saying, 'Tate Modern Only Accepts Mad People If They Are Dead'. I did wear it when I went to the Tate Modern to see the Robert Frank collection and was stopped from entering unless I covered the T-shirt. "You obviously want to make trouble", the security guard said. No, I just wanted to express my opinion. Thank you, Tate Modern, for telling me I am not allowed to express my opinion. I will bear that in mind.

This isn't the only instance Tate Modern has been bullies. There was another instance where an artist running a workshop at the Tate was told to leave to make way for some bankers to have their event. Money and arse-licking seem to come before art. Well, at the Tate anyway.

The irony of course is that they say we are too mad to be taken seriously and too mad to enter the building, but if you removed all the mad painters and writers off the walls of gallery and books off the shelves you'd be looking at empty walls and Catherine Cookson, and most major art organisations will discriminate while the mad artist is alive and exploit their talent when they are dead.

Before I came to Creative Routes, I was naïve as to how deeply society's prejudice of mad people ran. It has made me radical. It is a radicalism that is an acknowledgement that we are reacting to a society that is scared of us and will hijack our art and literature once our artists and writers are dead and therefore deemed safe and easy to control, corrupt and capitalise.

The discrimination we encountered with Tate Modern wasn't a one-off unfortunately. We have had it from other places, even major mental health charities or organisations. I know passionate people who stand up for their right to be treated with equality is a nuisance to society in general. Tough titties. We are already an alienated sector of society, in fact the most alienated sector of society. We are not full members of this society or culture and that is not going to change without us changing it. Because why is it in their interest to change what makes them feel comfortable and superior. Where does madness fit in 'normal culture'? We are the untouchables. Only fit enough to work in sheltered workshops, to be cleaners, media scapegoats and to paint multi-million pound masterpieces.

Creative Routes started to take over my life. It was such a life-affirming, energetic organisation and a joy to work for. I knew Creative Routes would one day have legendary status among the mad world, like Mad Pride, and it was very exciting to be one of ones right there at the beginning to help shape it. It was a magical time.

I took a break from Creative Routes to go to Amsterdam to do some poetry gigs arranged by Barry. His books were still not ready, but we did have were proof copies, so we tried to sell them.

I flew over and met Barry at the airport. Jennifer Acuri, an American poet living in Amsterdam with her Dutch boyfriend kindly let me stay at her place. She just left her highly-stressful, soul-destroying job and was finding her feet again. I think she will do that because she has already found her heart, she is such a kind, wonderful person. Her place was lovely, a huge place by Amsterdam's standards, covering three floors, with a spiral staircase. My first night in Amsterdam was just chilling out on Jennifer's rooftop terrace, and then having a meal.

The next day I met a lot of Barry's friends, and they were all remarkable people. One of them was Mathius who worked at Waterstones and who hosted the Radio 100 show. He is a really cool guy that belies the myth that Holland is a tolerant country. On his radio show he tells people what they don't want to hear about but should, and he gets beaten up for it. His daughter's beautiful poem was included in Barry's book.

He introduced us at Waterstones in a bright yellow jacket. The event wasn't well publicised, so most of the audience were just browsers off the street who were taking advantage of Waterstone's 2 for 3 book offer. Barry went into frenetic poetry about the madness of the world. The poor customers were very bemused. When Barry pointed out customers, they slipped out the door when he was not looking.

We did two gigs at Waterstones that day, one in the morning and one in the afternoon, accompanied by Vera, a friend of Barry's, who played classical guitar. While I was performing, Barry told Vera to tone down the music because they were overriding the words. She took offence and sneaked off when Barry was not looking. It seemed to me a lot of people did that to poor Barry – sneak off when he was not looking. When he turned around to introduce Vera, she was gone! "Where's Vera!" So he did some more poetry at the same time a melee of Hare Krishna went past the shop. They stopped near the entrance and chanted loudly for about 10 minutes. An exasperated Barry said, "How can I compete with that?"

As the gig wound up to a close, Mathius presented me with some flowers for 'publishing the lost souls of this world'. I was really touched by that. It made up for the fact that most of our audience were mystified tourists who wanted to escape us!

The highlight of that trip was going to Ruigoord. Ruigoord is an artist colony outside of Amsterdam. It is in middle of nowhere, out in the sticks, its neighbours huge multinational complexes looking sinister in the sparseness and silence of Holland's quieter corners.

Ruigoord was the closest thing I've ever come to a hippie commune. Outside open fires burned around painted buses, tents and teepees, and prayer flags draped across trees. Dogs without collars trotted about.

The main area of activity for the festival was the main church. It was huge, dark, crumbling on the outside, and full of stoned people on the inside. As the day's light got deeper, the haze of cigarette and pot smoke rose to the beams. I got something to eat and then went into the church to await the festival's start.

Inside, I sat at a table. Nearby was a man, he looked like a rockabilly, wearing a dark jacket and burgundy shirt. He had beer bottle in hand, beer bottle in soul. He staggered over to our table whilst Barry was rolling a joint. Barry pointedly ignored him. Barry left to do something and the guy proceeded to tell Jennifer and I how he liked to rape fruit – especially tomatoes. To debate the point that tomatoes were not a fruit seemed pedantic. I hoped he was joking. I still don't know if he was joking. But he was very perceptive about human nature – he got people's characters in a shot. Jennifer liked the pendant around his neck. He took it off for her to examine, "Otherwise you may have to touch my beautiful body." He said. Barry told me to ignore him, that he was one of the many hanger-ons the commune had.

It was an exquisite time and probably one of the highlights of my poetic career. My skin was made of clouds and my heart was the sun. I never feel my emotions in half measure, and this experience overwhelmed me. I didn't think for a minute my poetry would take me overseas to perform on the stage with poetry legends, such people like Simon Vinkenoog, who once performed at the Royal Albert Hall with Allen Ginsberg. Everyone was friendly to me, except certain poets who were pissed off at the world which didn't recognise their self-perceived genius, and expected me to bow down at their feet. These people are makers of their own loneliness. But I left them to their own self-made hell. They didn't detract from what was an unforgettable day.

On the last day of my trip to Amsterdam, I just walked around the city in the soft sun and stopped for coffees at cafes to people watch. On my last night I met Barry in a café. I was early and was harassed by an old white-haired guy, with a hearing aid. He took my hand and shook it for about 7 minutes the way drunks do; they give your arm a workout. Then he started kissing my hand and drawling drunken Dutch. I don't like turning my back on humans. But because of my alcoholic father, I am never easy around drunks. I couldn't understand what he said but I could tell he was a poet. I pulled my arm away and he moved on. It was a bar café for writers and journalists. I met and talked to a Dutch writer – I forget his name – about that there is no such thing as coincidence and whatever you positively will into being does happen. It can't help but do so. Once you have the thought and then the belief, watch the world bend over backwards to accommodate and salute you.

Back to London to continue to watch my dreams come true. My heart was my elevation. My feet couldn't touch the ground. The Scarman Trust grant came through to put on my play and I scouted around for venues. I chose the Nettlefold Hall Theatre in West Norwood, mainly because it was the nearest venue to me.

Then I found out I won a poetry competition and was going to be given a prize by Andrew Motion, the Poet Laureate. Wow, things were getting better, but things were not perfect. I think because of my enormous workload, things in my head were playing psychotic hopscotch. I know I wanted to make up for lost time. I was not used to working so intensely for such a sustained period of time, and I didn't as yet know what my limits were. My auditory hallucinations were increasing, my sleep was very disturbed, and I had periods of hypomania. I thought I could fly and was telling people I was going to go America without a passport and that it would only take 10 minutes to get there. I thought I could dematerialise and materialise anywhere in the world, as if I were in Star Trek.

This precarious frame of mind was complicated by the fact I was falling in love with Sarah. Everyone who knows her will testify to what a special person she is. She will disagree because she is very self-effacing. She says of me that I have a magnetic personality and that people are drawn to me, that there is something about me that is out of the ordinary. But I see that of her too. Our mutual friend, Melanie, a fellow mad chick, amazing artist and beautiful person, saw her at Mad Prider Robert Dellar's leaving party at Southwark Mind and said I have to get to know that woman. I thought the very same thing when I saw her for the first time.

She is a usual looking woman, tremendously beautiful, with gorgeous huge, exceptionally expressive eyes. She is dark haired and I correctly guessed by looking at her, she was of Jewish heritage. She is very hard to ignore, she is adorned and decorated by beautiful and colourful chaos, ribbons and bags trail behind her. There is no pretence about the woman, you know what emotion she is in when she is in it. She is honest almost to a fault. I have tried telling her some people need lying to; they are not able to take the truth comfortably. But she is just unable to lie, she has no editing facility between her brain and her mouth, which has got her into trouble many times. Her timekeeping is the worst of anyone I have ever met. She has no concept of time which makes appointments difficult. When I first met her, she stood me up twice. I stood two times outside the Maudsley where we arranged to meet, looking like a Naanaa. She said she would come to meet me with her aid dog Gem, so I went up to women with dogs, saying, "Are you Sarah?" The hospital security guard must have thought I was pestering these women, because he came out to check on me several times!

Ordinarily I would have nothing to do with a person that had stood me up twice, but my instinct, my gut reaction was to persevere and meet this woman. Had I known then how this woman would turn my world upside down both personally and artistically, I probably would have thought twice about meeting her, but I would have done it anyway.

I say in my last book that I wouldn't indulge in gay relationships because it would complicate my already convoluted life. Well, it is easy to make decisions about your life, it is harder to road test them. No decision huge or small can stand up to the power of falling in love, and that I did, and the decision I made seemed the silliest in the world.

But I didn't fall in love with Sarah overnight. We became colleagues first, then friends. Our phone calls to each other were a just a few minutes to begin with, talking about Creative Routes business. Then we talked about ourselves as well. We are both crazy about dogs. Sarah's dog Gem is a rescue dog from Battersea Dog's Home. She is brown and tanned, with fluffy ears with blond highlights! Look into her eyes and you see slightly cross-eyed magic, and know that angels can be in any form. Totally wonderful, totally crazy. She nods her head whenever she wants food, and she loves her grub. So we talked about our dogs. Then one awful day, out of the blue, I lost my dog Bobby to an epileptic fit. He was a magnificent rascal, always up to no good. He was a serious dog in his youth, and then in his old age became totally silly, where he would have fights with tents and help my dad feed the pigeons. So I was devastated when he died. Sarah was there for me, offering support and kind words.

She had come out of a relationship with a man so I didn't think for a second she would be into women, so I kept my feelings to myself, and anyone who has been through something similar will bear witness to what an exquisite turmoil it is.

Camberwell Arts week came and I was kept busy. I was part of a debate 'Without mad people, where would the arts be?' It could have been a stimulating debate, but apart from the actor Mat Fraser, everyone else was hopelessly White and Middle-class, so the talk was dry and pointless, passion frowned upon. A couple of them suffered that horrid middle-class disease: 'Discrimination? What discrimination?' I don't know how the audience managed to stay awake throughout it. I nodded off near the end.

That same week I collected my prize from Andrew Motion and read from my poetry book. Then off I went to the South London Gallery to do a poetry reading there. I had written poetic responses to the exhibition there by artist Tom Friedman, which included a huge blue model of a man looking at toy soldier size figure and a hairball dangling from the ceiling. The hairball had a security guard attached to it who spent most of the day telling people not to touch the hair. Surreal, yup, and I wrote about it in a couple of poems.

THE BIG BLUE
When I first saw the big blue guy
Looking down on the tiny person who was looking
Up to him, my first thought was – aha, the spectre
Of psychiatry, a huge body intruding on my space,
Looking down, looking down on people,
Looking but not seeing.

But the more I looked, the big blue guy softened, I noticed
He was slouched over, trying to make himself look
Smaller than he was, trying to make himself invisible

But that's not going to happen
Like trying to own clouds, or hoping
One bowl of cereal is going to last forever

It isn't going to happen.

The little person was looking at the giant like an exhibit in a
Freakshow, and now I am adding to the audience
There is nowhere to hide
For him
Or any of us.

ODE TO SECURITY GUARD GUARDING HAIRBALL
Ode to guy guarding hairball
Thank you for telling me it is art
I would have stepped on it, or
Picked the thing up, thinking it was rubbish
Thanks

The hectic summer was drawing to a close but I hadn't quite finished yet. My mental health was deteriorating somewhat, the highs falling far and painfully into lows, where I wanted to escape the skin I was in. I wanted to run away from myself but couldn't. I should have taken a month or two to recuperate but I was driven by a need to make up for lost time, that any second I didn't fill with productive activity would hate me and shred my skin and swallow me whole. I battled on, not knowing quite what I was fighting for.

Things were made worse by the fact I was feeling terrible abdominal and back pain because of gall stones. I had a scan at St Thomas which diagnosed that as the reason. I felt sick all the time and was in pain. I was put on a waiting list for an op, being told it could take up to six months for that to happen. The energy I usually used to struggle and tussle with my mental distress was being diverted into contending with the physical agony. I'll put it into perspective for you: quite a few women who have had gallstones and had children said giving birth was *less* painful. My dormant self-pity was collecting all this as ammo.

I would put a 12 hour a day into my work, constantly in physical agony and not eating. The weight was starting drop off of me. I didn't know how to slow down. Working for Creative Routes was seductive but exhausting. It would always offer me amazing experiences even though I was wasting away in mind and body.

For example, there was the time we did a performance piece for the Sainsbury Centre. The Sainsbury Centre for Mental Health is a charity, apart from research and development, organises conferences for those interested in mental health issues, mainly professionals.

In July 2004 we were invited to perform at one of their conferences about values at the New Connaught Rooms in Holborn, West London. We based the performance piece on challenging labels, which I directed.

Imma Maddox, one of our more eccentric members, is a proficient weaver and she had a trunk of these wonderfully weird weaved costumes, some of which had cloth penises. Because they were unusual, they were ambiguous – you sometimes didn't know which way up they were – so some people had penises coming out of their chests or shoulders!

So thus dressed we invaded the prestigious hotel full of suits.

Before we went on to perform we were put in the hall where the refreshments were served. There we had a table exhibiting leaflets and artwork by Creative Routes, womanned by Sarah. As I was feeling a bit sick and headachy I went under the table for a nap. Whilst I was under there I heard Sarah flirt with a Scottish male nurse. "You must be at least 6ft 3," I heard her say. I thought: oh, I must have a look and see. So my hand came out from under the tablecloth and grabbed his ankle. He wasn't at least bit fazed by my being under the table and held a conversation in this manner. I asked him if he knew Wishaw in Scotland, where my mum is from. He did. Grabbing ankles was so much fun I continued to do it to unsuspecting passer-bys.

We were told by the people organising the conference not to swear or insult psychiatry in any way. Oh, dearie me, Sainsbury Centre, I thought to myself, there wasn't going to be any of that but now there will be. Don't tell us what to do, don't remind us that our voices aren't listened to, and that our justifiable anger at psychiatrists should be censored so the ones in the audience won't be put off their sandwiches.

The live art piece began with a haunting beat from our Drum Circle, with 2 passer-bys ignoring a person in distress. In the end the only 'help' we get from professionals is a label and the discrimination that inevitably follows. So we live up to our labels, our voices not heard, and embarrassed to be alive. But as the live art moves on, we find our voices and our identities, and dispense with our labels. The piece was rounded off by us singing Bob Marley's 'Get up, Stand up!' to very stony-faced professionals with crossed arms high in their chests. We invited this audience to come up and dance; they didn't. I think the sticks up their arses made it difficult for them to participate. Those poor disabled people, disabled by their assumptions on mental health. We were an anarchic crew of amazing creatives, fiercely proud of ourselves, who refused to see ourselves as powerless or as poor little things that needed the 'help' of these professionals. The balance of power switched during that performance: they didn't know how to take it, and they didn't like it.

Sharing the performance space, just before we went on, was Louise Pembroke, who edited a book on self-harm. Her piece was a wonderfully graceful dance but before she went on she said to the audience, 'any of you who take holidays from pharmaceutical companies should be ashamed of yourselves.' I like this woman, I thought to myself. All the mad performers and speakers on that day were special. One speaker, a Black woman who came up and danced with us when we invited people on stage to celebrate our creativity with us, said something that has since stuck in my mind, "Mental Health care should so much more than it is. A lot of mad people were abused as children. Can you honestly say that psychiatric medication can heal abuse?"

I had invited Barry, my poet friend from Amsterdam to participate with us and earn some much needed cash from himself. He is as mad as a hatter without it being a psychiatric thing. Good old Barry, he both swore and insulted psychiatrists and it was music to my ears.

After the performance lunch was provided. The delegates got warm, delicious, filling meals and the performers got a few soggy sandwiches and some packets of crisps. I had to leave early for another appointment, so what happened next was related to me by Barry. Basically there was a food mutiny: first there was a protest to the organisers led by the Creative Routes posse and Louise Pembroke. They pointed out the irony that this was a conference focussing on values, and that the mad people got inferior food. The upshot of the incident was that the cake trolley was acquisitioned – nobody separates mad people and cakes and gets away with it! The Sainsbury Centre never spoke to us again. Everyone there from Creative Routes affectionately terms the incident 'Insanesbury' and we look upon it with fondness.

The myth of CR was beginning to weave its presence into the mental health world.

Less radical but just as much fun was performing at the Royal Festival Hall. We took part in Rhythmsticks, which is one of Europe's most prestigious drumming and percussion festival that runs yearly at the RFH. We were asked to take part in the Bang On The Hall event with Evelyn Glennie, the world-renowned percussionist. We had a series of workshops under the superb guidance of composer Tim Steiner. It was the first time I picked up a pair of drum sticks and I was nervous but by the time the event came around, I was bashing away with the enthusiasm of Animal from the

Muppets. Our percussion was the RFH foyer itself, the tables, the chairs, the walls, the railings, and the bins, everything that could make a sound. At the end of the performance we were all given a bouquet of flowers each. I left the South Bank on a high. I saw angels dancing on the Thames. I was living my dreams. Dreams are the only things not corruptible by society. Not dreams that are of human desire like I want to be an airline pilot, but the ones that burst through your sleep, and laughs at the day left behind. Saint Banality carousing with mischievous gods.

Being normal was boring and painful. My mind wanted to fly, every thought was a balloon heading for the sky and stars, but I was having to pull it down every second of every day of every year to converse and commune with the ordinary day. Just imagine a balloon filled with helium that naturally rises and having to pull it down again and again and again, so as not offend those without a balloon. During those times I was carrying an exhausted, weighted body and a flyaway weightless mind.

After Camberwell Arts Week, I signed up to be a volunteer for Mad Chicks, the newly established girly section of Mad Pride and then dove into my play 'Acts of Madness'. Acts of Madness is a short play about a psychiatric patient who can see the theatre audience but the psychiatrist insists it's a delusion. It's a cheeky play about reality in that it turns the audience into part of a delusion, or a madness that was not there to start off with.

I choose actors I already knew to play the parts. A couple a weeks from rehearsal I was let down by one actor, but that brought a blessing in itself in that I found a much better actor for the part. Devon Marston, a reggae musician, actor and worker with Sound Minds, a studio based in Wandsworth for people with mental health problems, focusing primarily on music stepped perfectly into the shoes of the character. A tall, gangly Black man, softly-spoken, I sent him over the script and he said to me, "I want to do this, the writing is brilliant!" He was going to play Jesus/Mike, the friend of Dana, the main character of the play. Devon loved that the guy he played thought he was Jesus, because he had similar experiences. He brought such humour to his part, that he had me and the other actors cracking up all the time. The other actor were Lloyd Lindsay, an amazing performance poet; O'Matsu-Hana Ramsoondar, a livewire of a woman, William Ball, a newcomer to acting, and Ali Kemp, who was at drama school at the time.

The first rehearsal at Inspire, which is in the crypt of St Peter's Church on the Walworth Road, Devon got lost so Jesus didn't come to save the day. Poor Jesus got stuck in Elephant and Castle! It was only the second time I directed stage actors so I was a bit nervous, but as rehearsals progressed, my confidence as director grew. I booked the Nettlefold Hall in West Norwood for the production.

The play was a black comedy posing very serious questions about what sanity is. The tagline of the play was 'Who is directing this production called reality?'

Here it is:

ACTS OF MADNESS was performed at The Nettlefold
Theatre in August 2004.

ACTS OF MADNESS (C) Dolly Sen 2004

OPENING SCENE:

INT PSYCHIATRIC WARD TV ROOM DAY

DANA is the only person in the room. She watching TV
and looking bored.

MIKE/JESUS, a fellow patient comes into the room.

MIKE/JESUS
What's on TV, Dana?

DANA
The same old shit.

MIKE/JESUS
I went into the kitchen to
see what we're having for lunch.

DANA
What are we having?

MIKE/JESUS
Macaroni cheese. I'm gonna head back in
there and make sure I have enough for the
5000.

DANA
Good one, Jesus.

MIKE/JESUS leaves the room and bumps into the
nurse coming into the room.

NURSE
Awright, Mike!

MIKE/JESUS
It's Jesus, man!

NURSE
Dana, your psychiatrist wants to see you.

DANA gets up half-heartedly.

SCENE CHANGE:

INT PSYCH WARD OFFICE DAY

DANA enters and slumps into a seat.

PSYCHIARTRIST
How are you, Dana?

DANA
Bored out of my mind. I want out of this
ward. I want to go home.

PSYCHIARTRIST
When you're better... Do you still think people
are watching you?

                    DANA
People are watching me. How can you not see
          them? They are right there!

She gets up and goes over to directly face the
audience, and picks out the characteristics of audience
                    members.

                    DANA
How can you not see them? There's a woman
in red there. And a bloke over there in a dodgy
                    toupee.

                PSYCHIARTRIST
            There is only a wall there.

                    DANA
Yes, a wall you built. They are watching my
              every move.

                PSYCHIARTRIST
              Why's that, then?

                    DANA
            I dunno. Ask them.

She goes into audience and points to one person.

                    DANA
      Look, here's someone. Ask them.

                PSYCHIARTRIST
            There's no one there.

I want you to get better and feel better, so I
am going to increase your medication.

DANA
No, I don't want more medication. It makes me
feel sick and messes up my vision. Do drug
companies give you commission or something?

The Psych looks at the mug he raised to his lips; it is
emblazoned with a drug name. He quickly puts it
away.

PSYCHIARTRIST
(ignoring her)
Don't be silly. We want you to feel better.

DANA
It seems to me I'm taking the medication to make
you feel better.

PSYCHIARTRIST
You can leave now.

DANA gets up and looks into the audience and
gestures the psych is crazy. The shrink doesn't even
look up.

SCENE CHANGE:

INT PSYCH WARD TV ROOM DAY

DANA is in the TV room again, curled up in a chair.

MIKE/JESUS
Not watching TV?

DANA
It's these drugs, man. They make my vision
blurred. I can't watch TV, can't read, can't write,
can't do anything.

MIKE/JESUS
No worries – I'll heal you.

He goes over to DANA and lays his hands on her
head. A NURSE enters the room.

NURSE
Mike, leave her alone!

MIKE/JESUS
I'm only healing her.

NURSE
Come on, Dana, your psychiatrist wants to
see you.

DANA
Later, Jesus.

MIKE/JESUS
See ya, Dana.

SCENE CHANGE
INT PSYCH OFFICE DAY

PSYCHIARTRIST
How are you, Dana?

DANA shrugs.

PSYCHIARTRIST
Can you see anyone watching you?

DANA squints towards the audience.

DANA
No, I can't see anything.

PSYCHIARTRIST
Don't you feel much better now?

DANA
(flatly)
Yeah, great.

PSYCHIARTRIST
If this progress continues, you'll be able
to leave soon.

DANA
(sarcastically)
Thank you.

She gets up and leaves the room. The psychiatrist
faces the audience.

PSYCHIARTRIST
It's amazing what some people see.

SCENE CHANGE:

The nurse takes Dana to the consulting room again.

Spotlight on a woman sitting on a chair, head in hands.

DANA
I keep hearing voices, horrible voices
that won't shut up. They keep going
on and on and on…

The light widens to include a psychiatrist on her left,
stuffed and uppity, with clipboard and pen.

PSYCHIATRIST
That's why I'm here, to help you get rid of these
horrible voices.

DANA
Then what are you doing still sitting here?

PSYCHIATRIST
Are you hearing a voice right now?

DANA
Of course, (she stares at the psych)
I can hear you loud and clear, and
as usual you are talking a bunch of bullshit.

The light widens further to include the woman's
madness. A person, slouching on a chair, looking
bored, wearing a T-shirt saying: MY MUM WENT TO
SANITY AND ALL SHE GOT ME WAS THIS LOUSY
T-SHIRT

VOICE
Yeah, tell him. Tell him he's talking rubbish as usual.

PSYCHIATRIST
I'm only here to help you. We just want
what's best for you.

DANA
Best for me? Best for me? Locking me up is
best for me? Drugging me so much that
you turn me into a zombie is helping me?
Do you really expect me to live the rest
of my life as a zombie?

VOICE
Yeah, tell the bastard. Why
are you even having a conversation
with this idiot?

DANA
(looking at the VOICE)
Will you shut up! I can't hear myself think!

PSYCH
Obviously you're still not well, so I'm
going to increase your medication.

DANA
No, no!

VOICE
Listen to me, I'm the only one that
cares for you. I can make you God
or a Queen, I can give you magical powers
– you'll be able to read minds. What do

you prefer to be? God or a queen? Or always
subservient to these arseholes. You can never be
more than a set of symptoms to them, a piece of shit
on their shoes.

DANA
I know that!

VOICE
When doctors remove a cancer, they
look on it with disgust. The cancer in you
is you, baby – to them.

DANA
(forcefully)
No more medication. Is the best you
can give my pain a sedating drug, so I
won't be much of a nuisance to you
and the rest of society? How about
improving my quality of life and getting
me out of the slum I live in? Or letting
me leave the ward once in a while, I'm sick
of staring at these 4 walls. Well, 3 walls
and an audience.

PSYCHIATRIST
Audience? Not that again. You
are obviously sick. I know what's best.
It's dangerous to listen to voices that hurt you.

DANA
My point exactly.

PSYCHIATRIST
We need to damp down these voices.

The drug you were on did that, why
did you stop taking it?

DANA
I haven't laughed or cried in years on these drugs.

PSYCHIATRIST
Don't you worry, we'll make being human a psychiatric
disorder.

VOICE
Ha, ha! That guy cracks me up. This is guardian
of reality, the teller of ultimate truth? What a joke.

PSYCH
Listen to me.

VOICE
Listen to me.

Dana turns her head side to side to listen to them.
Soon she is shaking her head violently. Dana then
springs from her chair.

DANA
That's it! I've had it with the both of you.
Where is MY voice in all this? I'm outta here.
I can't listen to you. I need to know what
my own voice sounds like.

PSYCHIATRIST
You can't do that! You have to stick to the script.

VOICE
Yeah, stick to the script!

DANA
Piss off!

PSY AND VOICE:
(together)
Boy, does she like the sound of her own voice.

PSYCHIARTRIST
Don't worry, nobody will listen to her.

The Voice nods.

DANA
I'm going to listen to my own voice.

She walks from the consulting room to the psych ward
TV room.

DANA
This is madness

Back in the consulting room:

VOICE
Wanna game of chess?

He puts a chessboard on the vacated chair.

The Psy nods.

PSY
The games people play, eh?

THE PERFORMANCE OF THE POEM 'THIS IS
MADNESS' by 'Jesus'. He is dragged away by a
nurse.
SCENE CHANGE:

DANA enters the TV room and sees a dosed-up
Jesus.

DANA
Jesus?

JESUS
Hey, Dana.

DANA walks over and sits down next to him.

DANA
What happened to you?

JESUS
Fucking hell, they dosed me up.

DANA
Do you feel any different? Do you feel cured?

JESUS
Ha! The cure is to make me too tired, too weak to do
anything.
The medication has made my mind so foggy
I have no idea what to do next. I know I have to do

something important. Was it save the world? I can't
remember any more. I'm going to end up just like my
deadbeat dad.

DANA
Yeah, my medication has turned my life into one long
side effect too.

JESUS
Why haven't left this shithole? I thought you were
allowed to go home.

DANA
Because I don't really have one. It's a mad world out
there. We're thrown into a community that couldn't
care less. I want nothing of it.

JESUS
So are you going to stay here then?

DANA
No, forget that.

JESUS
So where do we go from here?

DANA
I'm thinking of ending it all.

JESUS
Can you really cross the line though?

DANA
Yes, I've had enough drama in my life. I want out.
I mean, where else can I go?

MIKE/JESUS shrugs.

DANA
Do you want to come too?

JESUS
No, I'm waiting to be crucified. When are you
going to cross the line?

DANA
There's no time like the present.

DANA gets up and walks towards the audience. She
pauses thoughtfully at the line she has to cross, before
stepping into the audience and joining them. She sits
with them and says: 'What are we watching?

I decided to give away the tickets for free. The months
leading up to the play, I had given away 200 tickets, so
I had high hopes. A lot of the tickets went to mental
health professionals, including psychiatrists. Sarah & I
had fun on the phone planning a Sectioning of the
psychiatrists in the audience, only releasing them if
they sang us a song.

On the night the performances were magnificent but
there was a low turnout of audience, only a quarter of
the free tickets came to watch the play. I was hugely
disappointed. I felt I let my actors down and my ego
had a bruising. The mistakes I made were that I didn't

send ticket-holders a reminder of the play the week before. Some of the tickets went out months ago, so people could have simply forgotten it was on. Also the Nettlefold Theatre was hard to find. I did get emails later from people that they were unable to find the venue. I definitely learned from the experience but that didn't take the hurt away that the performance played mostly to empty chairs.

The people that did come gave me glowing reviews of the play. Niki Mylonas, a journalist, gave radiant review of 'Acts of Madness', saying "Let us hope Mindfull Productions and Creative Routes will continue to enlighten the ignorant and fill the planet with their unique talents and powerful voices."

Most of the front row was filled by Creative Routes members, they were fast becoming my new family. But even that couldn't penetrate my depression and disappointment. I had come a long way from being a negative person, but I was then still prone to bouts of self-pity and I did mope for a few days afterward. I did ultimately come out of it but for a long while I kept prodding the emotionally bruising of that experience and maintaining the discolouring of my soul.

What I've learned now is to take time out to examine and take apart my self pity to see how ridiculous it is essentially. But instead, at the time, I took my usual route of working so hard that my mind didn't have time or space to alight on the thorns that needed pruning.

What I eventually realised was that although I made mistakes with the project, I learnt from that, and didn't make the same oversight again. I can't remember which famous inventor said this, but he said something like after making over 1000 attempts on his invention: 'I haven't made a mistake, I have just learned a 1000 ways of not doing things.' It is better to have that take on life. Because it is easy for humans to think that perceived failures in what you do translate into being a failure as a human being. Which quite a jump but in this society it is conditioned into us that what you do is what you are. And if you don't produce, you lose your value. I have stopped living my life to the standards that a capitalist society has put down, a society that is digging its own grave. I live my life as a spiritual, learning process. I am not political in the slightest in that I don't subscribe to any party – because I believe the only effective change is internal change – it can't be forced from the outside. We must ask why mental illness is on the increase, why depression is going to be the number one health problem in the world in ten years time. I say is it any wonder in the society we are living, that asks so much and give so little? That asks us to be satisfied with life solely on the premise of producing and consuming, that does not give us time and space to know ourselves and each other, that doesn't let us **live** our lives?

Well, anyway, what audience was there absolutely loved it. I knew that there would be a fair number of mental health professionals, and I did wonder how they would take the play because it does take the piss out of psychiatry. Although one or two squirmed, I had encouraging feedback from the professionals; they wanted to see the play done elsewhere. I thought maybe in the future: I was more into film than stage but I wanted to say I had done a play and learn about the experience of writing, directing and producing a play.

Fast Forward grants gave Creative Routes some funding to do a mental health arts supplement that would be part of Artery, the magazine of Southwark Arts Forum. Part of the funding was training in desktop production, graphic design, and magazine production from Southwark Arts Forum. That didn't happen. It was one of our first inklings of how mercenary the 'real' world is. Southwark Arts Forum took the money and gave us almost no support and guidance. We had to put together the supplement ourselves. It wasn't the first time – or last time – Creative Routes was taken for a ride. If this is how sanity operates in the main, how dare you tell me – no, actually force me to be part of it.

But it was interesting and valuable experience. It gave me a chance to be a magazine editor, and my editorials pulled no punches. I think society has this perception that mad people are passive – or should be passive – and be grateful for being in the sane world. To expect equal rights and respect, believe it or not, is seen as being cheeky and part of our madness. And in our demand for respect we are intelligent, artistic, and passionate and that totally throws them. I didn't realise how timid we were expected to be. People expected a politically correct daycentre newsletter, what they got instead was criticism of Tate Modern and the disturbing art of Phil Lancaster's auditory hallucinations and paranoia. His amazing piece was called 'a camera in my head'. We also put in reviews of our events, and published poetry, cartoons, artwork and photography. Funding only allowed us to run for 3 issues but I was a better editor and journalist for it, and my disgust for the mercenary sane world was compounded. Innocence and goodness are seen as things to make you money and to exploit. Generally throughout my Creative Routes career, I have discovered that if you want to make positive change in society, you will be ripped to pieces. Because so many people profit from society being negative.

Injustice and discrimination is subtler nowadays. For instance, no need to burn books, or question validity of news coverage, provide mind-numbing reality TV and you have them in the palm of your hand. No need to worry about a Third World that is manmade, the running shoes it cheaply produces look good on you. No need to worry about pollution or the wars that come out of oil, cars represent freedom. And no need to castrate the mad, psychiatric drugs will render you impotent anyway. Discrimination is so prevalent if you are mad, nothing is untouched by it. If you go to the USA you have to declare if you have a mental illness; if you are a victim of crime, your testimony in court is meaningless; hundreds of psychiatric patients have died under 'restraint and control', how many people have been convicted of killing them – not a single one. Trying getting a job or insurance without lying.

The most disturbing of the previously mentioned are deaths under psychiatric care. This would not be tolerated in a general hospital but is seemingly justified in mental hospitals.

Something you notice in some newly qualified psychiatric nurses is that there is that compassion. But when they see their superiors and people longer in the job acting in a less than sympathetic way, they can either protest and be labelled a troublemaker and be ostracised, or they can follow suit, in such spurious procedures such as control and restraint. Luckily I haven't had that recently; the last time was as a teen. But in the cases I have witnessed in the last 7 years, it didn't need to happen. It happened because the staff member that perpetrated it was in a bad mood, or they saw it as a quick way to regain control. Talking the person down over a cup of tea, or just talking took too long, and expended too much mental activity. It is sad some nurses would rather indulge their laziness than act in a humane way that could actually help the person experiencing distress. I have been on the other side as a mental health professional. I have worked in a volunteer capacity with mental health organisations for over 10 years, with some very ill people whose distress caused them to be aggressive. I will not even consider restraint, unless they were about to commit suicide or harm someone else. Every time there has been aggression I have talked that person down and out of their aggression. Usually it ends with me hugging them, believe it or not. I do realise some nurses can't do that, they are just not that bright or caring. If that is the case, they shouldn't be in the job. Control and restraint should be the very, very last resort. That fact is it is sometimes used as the first line of action.

We also need to consider why these people become aggressive, and if it is aggression at all. Resisting medication because of its horrible side effects is not belligerence. It is a very reasonable response. Maybe their mental health would be better improved by talking therapies or better housing or social conditions. And there is that frightening concept that clinical judgement is not that but influenced by doctor's moral idiosyncrasies.

Why people become aggressive should be looked at. I bet common themes come up. Those themes should be tackled with as much force as the control and restraint itself. Then we will see welcome change. And not just bruises on the bodies of distressed humans. Or even worse, the headstones of those that have died because of it, such as Rocky Bennett.

Control and restraint can be as degrading as rape. And when I had it, it was painful. Days after I could still feel the grip on my arms.

Maybe change can begin with training for nurses, because they are taught to see the illness, the symptoms, the thing that is 'wrong' with the person. They are trained not to see the whole person.

The mental health system is defined by finance, and most of that finance seems to fund awful, soul-draining buildings and incompetent staff. And those poor under-resourced pharmaceutical companies need their slice.

On a fundamental level, psychiatry is built on a quicksand of things that do not exist. Nobody can define normality. Since the beginning of time, philosophers and the like have tried to define the mind, and nobody has got it on the nose yet. But psychiatry proposes to understand it. Go to a general hospital and you will see every part of the human body has a specialist department and staff dedicated to one part of the body. The mind is boundless, measureless, but there is just psychiatry to deal with the whole thing. What do they build in response to the mind? Padded cells and ECT machines to make sure it behaves itself.

Psychiatry is there to make sure we behave ourselves. It is not there to deal with trauma and pain, that is secondary.

There is this big black hole in psychiatry that no-one talks about much. It's called love. A fair majority of service users have had appalling upbringings, terrible abuse and neglect. They weren't allowed the right of love in childhood, and nor are they allowed the right of love in psychiatry. Love is seen as a dangerous thing. Boundaries and all that shit. Job description of professionals does not talk about love. Pharmaceutical companies are scared of it, they could lose millions of pounds a year if MH professionals gave honest love to their clients, or provided effective ways and means to tackle the loss of love in a life that needs love. Can a tablet cure abuse? Can a tablet replace loss of love? Can a tablet be a reason for living?

Also, it may be said, that love will reward dysfunctional behaviour, as if mental anguish is a thing that should be punished or rewarded for. Also love and bureaucracy don't mix. You can't build institutions on love. The mental health 'issue' is created by psychiatry. If we were to tolerate different thinking and to offer nothing but compassion to people in distress, where is the 'issue'?

Madness is a social/political product. This greedy, self-centred brutal society produces madness like it produces reality TV shows and shampoo. Say, as a paradigm that madness tomorrow can resolve the energy and environmental crisis, madness would be no longer viewed as an illness. Our value in society would escalate and people will want to be like us.

There is a painful side to madness but it makes you feel valued, it is an acceptable difficulty.

You have to see the history of madness to realise it has never been a static state, and has various definitions and reasons for being to reflect the society of the time. And it is telling that madness is always a dumping pot, a dustbin for whatever is 'wrong' with society at the time. In the middle ages you were mad because you were possessed by the devil. Then later on when the animalism of man was seen as the worse thing you could be, that was reason you were mad. It mostly has religious connotations but madness isn't exclusively a religious construct. More recently in our capitalist epoch, the mad person is despised because he or she is not a unit of production, so therefore there is something 'wrong' with being mad. This hasn't always been the case, the mad person wasn't always demonised, in ancient cultures the mad person was accepted within communities.

The trouble is psychiatry is about social control and not about providing hope. Apart from easing distress, I think the mental health system should be less about containment and control and more optimistic, a stronger belief in people's recovery and help people to develop their personal power.

Am I delusional for wanting this?

I only want to be friends of dreamers who want beauty to feel less ashamed of itself in this sometimes ugly world. One of my favourite dreamers contacted me. Barry wanted to do another tour with him.

Barry eats, drinks and shits poetry. I don't think it matters to the guy whether he makes a penny from his work, he will do it because he is passionate about poetry. He hadn't performed in the UK for years and wanted to do a tour. He decided to use the opportunity to introduce some legendary Dutch poets to the UK, and called it the Dutch Connection tour. He also got the best of UK talent, such us Luke Wright and Patricia Foster. It was a huge undertaking and he had to do it all himself. Us poets are not the easiest of people to please, and from the sounds of it, some of the poets expected red carpets and private jets. He had to juggle 30 poets, which of course gave him no time to do proper publicity. On top of that, Survivors Poetry promised some money to fund the tour, but as time, that water that burns, loomed closer, there was no cash, so Barry had to dip into his overdraft to fund the project.

Barry also comes from a beautiful naivety that if the poets are good, the collective consciousness will take note and people will turn up for gigs. He also put his trust into the venues we used to advertise the gig. The Custard Factory, for example, didn't even advertise the gig on their website. It is a rare poetic creature that can understand marketing. I did learn a lot on the tour about the necessity of marketing, and it is a sin I have learned to cultivate. As it turned out, only 10 people turned up for the Custard Factory gig, and two of those only came into use the toilet, Barry wouldn't let them go! It was not a wasted opportunity; I learnt so much and met some wonderful poets.

It also helped me hone my bullshit radar about who was in poetry for the love of words and who were in it for the love of fame. My favourite part of the tour was in Norwich - a town full of wonderfully weird people. We had a respectable audience size at the Norwich Arts Centre. I met a woman who was one of the acts at Glastonbury in recent years. She told me she had to pitch her tent in the dark; the tent didn't stay up very well. She woke up the next morning to find she tried to pitch her tent on the actual stage! She flirted with me and begged me to go back to her hotel room. I said no. Too tired. Too in love with Sarah. I ended up staying at Art Centre Manager's home, which used to be an ex-brothel, with a couple of other poets before heading back to London in a car owned by the lovely, crazy Liverpudlean poet called Roger Cliffe-Thompson, whom I met back in Amsterdam. We got lost, trying to find our way into London. At one point we drove for miles without seeing anyone, so we were overjoyed to see two Tibetan-looking men who were inspecting a lamp-post. Roger stopped the car to ask them for directions. I was in the car so I couldn't hear what they were saying. But the young Tibetan guys were shaking their heads a lot. Roger came back into the car with a scowl. "They can't speak English." As we drove away from them, I did wonder with bemusement, at what two Tibetans who can't speak English were doing in England, looking up a lamp post. Such are the mysteries of life.

I think one of the reasons I kept a full schedule was I didn't want to be alone with my thoughts. My feelings for Sarah were getting stronger. How cutting it is to feel an all-consuming love for somebody and not be able to tell them about it, lest they reject you and leave your life and give you a black hole bigger than all space and time in your life and still the love. Pouring love in a hole and feeling my heart break every time I thought of her.

I also did something without the necessary preparations and support to make it successful. I stopped my medication. The anti-psychotics I were on were so tiring to be on. It didn't give me enough energy to do the things that improved and maintained my quality of life. I was going to bed at a silly hour like 8pm. I felt like a child. I'd drop into bed with so many ideas, dreams and thoughts in my head, but a body to that couldn't fulfil those dreams. It also made me put on weight, and dribble at times. Psychiatric medication makes you look and feel like a second-rate human.

But coming off medication whilst I was in all this emotional and mental turmoil was not the right thing to do. I quickly became unwell. The beautiful angels of my hallucinations were beginning to talk behind my back. Paranoia was peeling off skin until my body was a pure open wound.

Then I got a phone call from Sarah in which she admitted she had similar feelings for me. Because she was also confused about a lot of things, there was bewilderment and disorientation still, but it felt nicer. Chaos with stars attached.

It was time to turn my attention to Mad Chicks. There were only a few of us organising the event we had planned for November but we did it. Apart from myself, there was Melanie Clifford, one of my best friends and a remarkable, incredible woman, an artist, a mad woman, and in one person a heart that has more love than the whole of psychiatry. I am blessed to have met her. The other included Mad Priders Gini Simpson, who works for Space Studios, an extraordinary woman who juggled work, child and commitment to ensure the rights of women in the mental health system. Esther Leslie was also one of the core group, another big heart and great mind. Sarah helped from a distance. Esther Wheatley, Rachel Studley, Penny Shaughnessy and Debbie McNamara also were pivotal in creating Mad Chicks, so we were a pretty astonishing bunch of women.

The event planned was going to be an information fair and workshops during the day and a wild gig of music, live art, comedy, film, poetry and dance in the evening.

When we told people in the system, namely men, they said why be a separate entity, why exclude men? I think Mad Chicks is necessary because the survivor world can be a chauvinistic one, and being female and mad has its unique issues that some men don't get and that needs more focus directed at it with a unified voice. As we say on our website: We believe the female service user voice has been overlooked as a positive strength. Some of the issues unique to mad women are things like mixed wards, childcare, assertiveness, rights, abuse and sexism in the NHS. I don't know a single woman who has been on a ward that has not been not been sexually harassed. I was sexually assaulted on a ward in 1999 and I know other women who have been raped. So it isn't a minor issue.

After a couple of funding letdowns, we were happy to get funding from Comic Relief and the Arts Council. It was really hard work preparing for the event, my first real taste in event management and promotion. I wrote the press release, amongst many other things. It was as follows:

'Piss off Prozac. Watch the great mad women of art, poetry and rock & roll give you a serotonin orgasm. MAD CHICKS, the girly section of Mad Pride, is about women psychiatric patients and survivors of the psychiatric system, who are sick of being treated like crap and generally sidelined.

Hearing voices?

MAD CHICKS gives a voice to those who are not listened to, or have had their voices taken away - a theft perpetuated in the much-hated new Mental Health Bill, which further demonises an already alienated section of society. MAD CHICKS gives that voice back with a scream. We say listen to the voices you're hearing, don't take these voices away with forced drugs.

We're launching MAD CHICKS in London, on Saturday November 27th 2004, 1-11pm at The Union Chapel, Highbury, North London.

The day is for women and girls only, and includes an info fair, creative workshops, debates, video, artwork, massage, and a café. The evening gig is for all genders: a glorious night of Music, Live Art, Comedy, Poetry, Film & Dance.

The line-up includes:

Gina Birch & Ana da Silva - Musicians who formed subtle, difficult, inspirational & ground-breaking all-female punk band The Raincoats will both be playing solo sets.

Maggie Nicols - Outstanding jazz performer in the European improvisation scene, notorious for her 'impossible vocal fireworks' Gertrude - Young all-female post-punk band. Plus over 10 other outstanding

and subversive acts enough to make you question
your sanity and then reject it!'

Some of us were worried nobody would turn up but I knew we would draw in a good crowd. One of the ways we promoted the event was to use a clear spot on Resonance Radio. On it we talked about being a female service user, read poetry and a piece on self-harm. The four of us on the radio show were allowed to choose two music tracks. I picked Lydia Lunch's 'Outpatients' and The Singing Nun's 'Dominique'!

On the day, because there was less than 10 of us, we all had about 4 roles each. Not only did I help set up in the morning, I was directing the filming, arranging the refreshments and holding a workshop on 'Creative Subversion' with Sarah. Poor Sarah was already exhausted before she even came to Mad Chicks. She told me she had woken that morning, with a half-eaten Crunchie stuck to her lips. She was so tired, she had fallen asleep while eating chocolate. My poor baby. She had forgotten to bring art materials and refreshments too. So it was a mad dash to the local supermarket. We zoomed around the shop, chucking food into our trolley. When I saw Sarah throwing in food into someone else's trolley, I thought, you poor thing, go home and get some sleep. We came back to the Union Chapel right on the dot for lunch. But our day wasn't over, in fact it only had just begun. Sarah and I had the Creative Subversion workshop to do.

Our workshop was the most popular of the event. Sarah and I made no preparations for it, except bringing our mischief and passion along. We started the workshop off by saying we belonged to no political party. Our politics were dictated by seeing suppression and prejudice and subverting it to our own advantage. We gave the only definition of creative subversion as just being ourselves and making our voice heard in a creative way. Gem stole the show by her gorgeous self. We talked about being discriminated by Tate Modern – we renamed them Tate Prehistoric for their backward thinking - and how we were going to embarrass Tate Modern by doing nothing more by holding up a mirror to their own stupidity.

We also talked about ECT and how we were going to bring it to an end. We also realised we could overturn so many regimes just by pretending to be incontinent old woman. The power of urine to change society shouldn't be understated.

Then it was the gig in the evening, which was incredible. I couldn't believe I was going to be on the stage with so many female legends. No wonder I find it hard to differentiate between dreams and reality when my waking life is the stuff of fantasies. It was heady and exhilarating; I did not feel my exhaustion until the next day.

There were a lot of gay and bisexual women at Mad Chicks, and what was talked about was the possibility of establishing an offshoot of Mad Pride called Mad Queers. I liked the idea but I had no physical energy to pursue it at the time but it is something I would like to do.

As with racial, gender and religious issues in mental health, sexuality needs to be addressed. There should be more LGBT professionals. Theoretically, the LGBT professional has a better understanding of the challenges and problems that being gay or bisexual in this society engenders. But primarily I don't look for a professional to be the same gender, sexuality or race as me. First and foremost I look for compassion, empathy. But *all* mental health professionals should understand what being different in this society entails.

I am bisexual. It used to be tempting to hide my gay side so I was more accepted by everyone, but when I did it I felt only half a person and not a truthful person. I also felt that there was part of me to be ashamed of. I thought: fuck it, Dolly, you can't be half a person all your life. Are you hiding to make bigots more comfortable; or worse more powerful? Verbal abuse I can take.

But there is a pressure for bisexual people to conform. I have had people say to me, well, you like men, why not just stay with them? It's less hassle, etc.

But one environment I would be scared to disclose my bisexuality is in a ward situation, especially a mixed ward. The men there are usually very macho, and a lot I have come across on the ward have been homophobic.

Like being on the receiving side of racism and sexism, homophobia is a painful prejudice to experience. To be abused or alienated in a society will have an adverse effect on your mental health. How can it not? It attacks who you fundamentally are. Just imagine the devastating effect of coming out to your family as Gay, Bisexual or Transgender and have them utterly reject you. You think: am I really that terrible, that unlovable, that my own parents hate me because of the gender of the person I love. So it is as no surprise that there are studies where it is recounted anywhere between 20-50% of LGBT people attempt suicide.

Each form of discrimination or prejudice has its own shape, and homophobia is unique in that prejudice can come from your own family, and in that way even more devastating.

Homophobia has lessened in my lifetime, thank goodness, but there is still a longer way to go. I am lucky when I came out to my family, they didn't blink an eye. I think they knew anyway.

It is hard also to be young and gay, especially if you don't have gay role models to help you through teenage landmarks that their straight counterparts take for granted like first crush, first kiss, first date, first sex, and so on. As non-straight people this is how we experience life and the mental health system. Staff of the mental health world need to understand this.

I didn't come out to everyone until I was in my 30s, so I think 'what guts' when I see an openly gay or bisexual adolescent. I say that because you know they are going to be bullied at school, and probably they are feeling they are the only ones. The suicide garden grows from the soil of isolation. It is not unexpected that there are high rates of suicide and attempted suicide in Gay youth.

As I write this book, there has been a local homophobic murder of Jody Dobrowski in Clapham. Being different can be lethal.

Homophobia can be subtle. Some mental health professionals don't want you to talk about it, and when you do you see the discomfort in their face and gestures. When you see that, then you yourself don't feel comfortable about talking about it, about something important in your life. You could be going through a rough patch with your partner but you keep quiet about it to the detriment of your mental health.

I have had professionals trying to change the subject. When I see that, I wonder if a gay or bisexual person's depression has arisen from their confusion about their sexuality and they wanted to talk it through with someone, how frustrated that must be and how it adds to the self-loathing some LGBT people have.

When I was in hospital on the Lloyd Still Ward, one of my named nurses had a chat with me. When she asked me about relationships, I told her I had broken up with my girlfriend. She patted my shoulder comfortingly and said, "Not to worry, eh, you are better off with a man anyway." Dealing with painful feelings with regards to a split was hard enough, but to get this reaction, which was not malicious but a vicious and arrogant compassion. I didn't sleep that night thinking how depressing it is that these people are caring for me.

I remember in 2004 I was with on the South Bank, chilling out with my girlfriend. We went home quite early. In next day's news the homophobic murder of a gay man was reported. He was killed a stone's throw to where I was cuddling my girl. Had we been there when they those wanker murderers were there, who is to know whether there would be someone writing this book now. So the threat is very real, and homophobia is still very dangerous. I have also had 'dyke' and 'batty' spat at me from cars.

Everyone knows what low self-esteem is. Can you imagine what the effect of being in a society that doesn't treat you as an equal member has on your mental health? Or seeing the pathetic outrage of prejudiced people taken seriously. I have lost count of the times that there has been anger that taxpayers or lottery money are paying for gay community groups. Gay people pay their taxes too, this is their society too. If you insist gay people have inequality in society, then maybe they should pay fewer taxes; that way they have value for money.

Or just imagine being in the closet, and having to lie to be accepted, or face the possible rejection of your friends and family. If that doesn't make you dejected, I don't know what will. Survey after survey shows that HIV is not the top health problem affecting gays and bisexuals – it is depression.

There is less homophobia than they used to be, but parents still prefer their children to be straight. Even if they don't outright reject you, there is that feeling of exclusion when parents talk proudly about straight children's partners and kids, and gay partners don't get a mention. I am very lucky with most of my family. My siblings don't have a problem with it at all. They can talk comfortably about my gay partners. My mum is also totally supportive, but I realise she has to contend with homophobia with her generation. When friends of my mum ask me when will I get married and have kids, or do I have a boyfriend, my mum gives me that look of 'don't say anything', so I don't.

I haven't told my dad. I think he would murder me in my sleep if he knew. He has said several times that gay people should be exterminated. But fuck that, dad, and fuck anybody else that thinks that. It says a lot about your morality and how much soul you have when you think mass extermination is less sinful or wrong that me loving someone of the same sex.

Just imagine the confusion and conflict you will feel from the ambivalence from your loving but homophobic family. You might wish you were straight not to have this worry, this sense of feeling like a lesser being.

We don't belong to one culture and one culture only, and we often inhabit cultures that conflict with each other – of course this causes mental pain. For example, I can't talk about my bisexuality with my family on my dad's side, because they are Indian and sexuality is a huge taboo in the Asian community, and they are also strict Christians. Because we all reside in many culture areas, the best thumb of rule, is to treat people with respect.

All forms of discrimination and prejudice are disturbing and demoralising. I am also biracial so racism has featured in my life. I came across racism at an early age. When I was about four we moved into Keymer Road in Streatham, the only non-white family on the street. As luck would have it, we moved right next door to the biggest racists on the street. They would spit at us and called us pakis. The White people on the street were very cold to us. This shaped my perception of the world as an unsafe, unkind place. The racism I endured I am sure in one of the myriad of spiked components that built my insanity. It made me a lost person, it made me feel that this world was not my planet. An outsider that didn't even realise that was an inside.

This was made more complicated in that I was biracial, not fully accepted by either race. Indians saw me as White, and Whites saw me as Indian.

I am aware of Mental Health Charities and research organisations looking into Black deaths in psychiatric care, and am surprised at the ethnicity of such panels, and the lack of Black people on them. It is racism with good intentions. I am sure these people genuinely wanted to help but they haven't really. If twice as many Black people are being forcibly restrained than White people in psychiatric care, then to disregard that it could be due to racism is naïve, but it is a naivety that is dangerous because more Black bodies will being leaving psychiatric care for good – in a casket. It is the same with gay issues. It is the same with user representation in mental health charities. Mind only has a quarter of its staff as survivors.

So how to restrain people is a bit more formulaic now. How they restrain people is looked into but why they restrain people is looked upon as secondary. It is the wrong way around.

Why are BME over-represented in acute wards?
Racism of the system plays a part, but the other reason is that because of cultural and language barriers, it is harder to go to the GP, and even if they

do go, because of these barriers it takes longer to communicate your distress to an overworked doc with only 10 minutes to spare you and that gets frustrated that you are not like him or her. And why would you want to go to the GP in the first place when in your culture madness has the hugest shame attached to it. And why would you go if the professional is critical of your culture. They may not say anything but you can sense it, you can feel it. So where the crisis could be averted in the early stages, it hasn't. So the services only see them when they are severely distressed and causing some kind of disruption.

Why do BME stay in the acute wards and services? Those who have been in the system longer know that they will get the worst services offered to them: the cheapest medication, and little in the way of therapies. So they become the lost of the lost, the underside of the bottom of the heap. I would be screaming and acting out to fight my way out of the hell around me. Psychosis is shattering and brutal. The psychiatric system should be counteracting that but is instead competing with the horror by offering the cruelty of mirrors for your paranoia. They will make your paranoia real. More so, if you are non-white and non-heterosexual.

It is further complicated for me, in that there is discrimination within discriminated groups. If you are mad too in ethnic and gay communities, you are looked upon as a disappointment. One thing I had levelled at me, "Don't you think we have a tough enough time being accepted, having you in our ranks just makes it harder." They didn't tell me to fuck off but I felt uncomfortable. It is alienation within alienation. It is a lot of weight to carry. And seeing sexism, racism and homophobia in the mental health system disturbs and hurts me. People tell me things are getting better but it's happening too slowly. It is a lot of wait to carry.

Where to begin? Well, cultural training should be mandatory for all mental health staff. When survivors are asked what would help them, they say people cited community-based culturally-based projects should be made more available. And people talking to media about their experiences so the public has a better understanding is essential.

The most powerful thing I can do is say I am mad, biracial and bisexual and I am beautiful and I amazing and I am free to be me. And nobody can make me feel small. I won't allow them to.

I can be made to feel like shit but I want to be a star. I talked a little about this when Creative Routes accepted an award. Creative Routes won an award from SELF, a charitable trust primary focused on regeneration. These awards were given to groups at the Southwark Snowball at the Bankside Gallery on the South Bank on the 10th December. Sarah, Gem and I, along with supporters, went to pick up the award. But we almost weren't there to receive it. Gem the dog, who everyone knows is the genius behind CR, wasn't allowed in. Natalie, of the Disability Rights Commission, stepped in and sorted it out. Gem was allowed to attend the awards ceremony.

One of Sarah's issues is anxiety and fear in social situations. The presence of Gem enables her to leave the house and engage with people. Her wonderful Dog

Gem makes her feel safe. If she didn't have Gem, Sarah wouldn't have an adequate quality of life. Going out would be an ordeal for her. So Gem is very much an enabling dog. Please tell me how she is not an enabling dog, because we are constantly being ejected from premises because small-minded security guards say she isn't one. Their judgement is based on ignorance of both mental health and the Disability Discrimination Act. I would love to hear a security guard give a presentation on disability because they are so obviously experts in the area. A lot of organisations aren't malicious but act out of ignorance.

The Snowball Event was full of important people from government and the local community. Sarah took this opportunity to network with them to ensure we got the desperately needed office space at Camberwell Leisure Centre. Gem also networked, primary with people who had food – I wonder why? My job on the day was guard duty and speech giver. Guarding because I was standing behind Sarah, hiding the hole in her trousers! I also wrote the following speech, although I didn't get to read the whole of it.

"You can do more than regenerate an area, you can regenerate people too. And Creative Routes have done that. I have seen members who, when they first joined, were so shy you hardly heard them speak, but grew to be confident because people cared for them and believed in them. For me personally CR has shown me the way to the stars.

Yesterday I read a quote, that went: 'Be humble, for you are made of dung. Be noble, for you are made of stars.' Because of a mental health diagnosis, you lose control of your life, you lose your worth and become a pariah in society. Creativity gives you that control back, it gives you back your worth. CR shows you the way from being seen as dung to being seen as stars.

There are people who have helped us on this route, the journey from dung to stars. Rachel from the South London Gallery got a star as did a few others.

Sarah handed out stars tied to ribbons to these amazing people as a thank you.

"Thank you, we have our own awards too for you. Please accept these stars, stars you have helped us become.
I just want to say one thing about social exclusion, I think it would really helpful for organisations to have mental health awareness training, because mental health disability is a hidden disability and people make all sorts of assumptions, and can discriminate unwittingly. The Disability Discrimination Act which came in this year makes that discrimination illegal in fact. But don't see the DDA from the viewpoint of doing something wrong, where you can get your hand slapped. See it as ways of improving the service you deliver, and being socially inclusive.

I am saying this because we were going to be excluded from today's event because certain people weren't fully understanding of certain mental health issues, which caused us distress actually, and really took the fun out of this event for us. Thankfully it was finally resolved, but we are constantly having this happen to us.

But thanks for the award, but we are more thankful for having the barriers removed that would have blocked our way here today."

After that, the latter part of 2004 wasn't as hectic but Our Creative Routes workloads made me and Sarah short and cranky with each other, and we started arguing. Sarah was totally committed to Creative Routes and the time we spent together that didn't have anything to do with Creative Routes was diminishing at an alarming rate. I was feeling jealous of the organisation. My insecurity augmented itself with every new project. I thought to myself, am I not more important than work? I made impossible demands on Sarah. Love was beginning to be the most excruciating thing in the world.

I said to several friends, things were so much easier when I was a loner. Being a loner protects you from love. When I was a loner and not connecting with the life, everything was a haze of unrecognisable emotions. But the valuable – and occasionally unwanted - thing being with people has done is rejuvenated my emotional life. I went from apathy to passion. So the good things in life feel excruciatingly beautiful. And the pain more vivid, stark and methodical. I have seen this by going through what every human being has gone through, a universal experience yet the pain and joy is so personal, I am watching in awe the circle of death and birth, the anguish of losing loved ones like my Scottish Nan, my Indian great-Aunt, my beautiful doggies - Bobby who died from an epileptic fit, Ginger from old age. I mourned heavily for my losses. Death turns love into torture but you can't stay tortured for long, because out of death and winter there is new life and spring. My sister Sheila has given birth to two absolutely gorgeous children. The love I have for them can't be touched by anything or anyone else. Hannah-Marie was born in April 2004, a red-head. When I saw her just a day old I marvelled at the sense that she wasn't new but a very old soul. She is growing up to be quite wonderful, there's something about her, a light in the eye that not many people share. At my worst, she can make me smile. The goldenness and warmth and purity that her small being holds has its magical effect on me. And now it is the same with Kallum, my nephew. Sometimes I can't stand the beauty of them and the love they bring up in me. You see in children humanity is absolutely perfectly fine. And the perfection is love without discrimination.

My love for Sarah was discriminative. She was an adult human. I didn't have a good track record with adult humans or with love - as anyone who has read my first memoir 'The World is Full of Laughter' will see. I projected these insecurities onto Sarah. Our relationship was slipping into co-dependency. I needed her to feel good and if she wasn't there, I was nothing and nobody. Very dangerous for both of us. My self-worth was tied up in her. That was too much of a burden for her to take. If she didn't ring me for a day, I didn't see the truth of the matter that she wasn't near a phone or wasn't well enough to ring. I thought she didn't ring because she hated me and that I did something to upset her. **I felt she was rejecting me when she wasn't. That is my biggest issue.** Perceiving rejection when there isn't any, and reacting like the hurt little girl I was emotionally. I was still that 5 year old who had been sexually abused and the whole neighbourhood and school knew had been, and ostracised accordingly, getting only pitying looks or rejection from people who couldn't handle it.

I talked to MH professionals about it and said I wanted counselling to deal with this issue that made love so painful, so fraught. They ummed and ahhed and said they couldn't really help. I thought about going to RELATE but they wouldn't work with people who have experienced psychosis. I was drowning. I became angry that the system has almost nothing for supporting mad couples through their rough patches. Mental Health Services had their head in the sand with regards to mad sexuality and relationships. They subscribe to the rampant and prevailing assumption that mad people are unlovable and that it is a lost cause to try and 'allow' them to have relationships. And aren't they impotent, anyway? Whenever I wanted a psychiatric professional to shut up I would bring up the request of relationship counselling, and they would go strangely and uncomfortably silent for a while. Some say love is madness and no psychiatrist can help. Because love is a madness that has no cure. And no psychiatrist can understand love or madness. That's why psychiatry is pointless. As my beautiful friend Paul Turner has said, "A psychiatrist is a person who can say to a highly suicidal person, "I'll see you next week." They just don't get it.

So I was drowning and didn't see the sun that Sarah truly was. Love stopped existing, and I didn't feel its warmth any more. I was incapable of feeling loved through the turbulence of insecurity and psychosis. Every time I thought of her, it brought a drop of kerosene to the skin, until I couldn't go out into the sunshine without self-immolating.

2005 came into being. I knew I was going to go mad or commit suicide in it.

<u>2005</u>

I am escaping from hell. From a tortured world into my art. Art is all that is, remaking the universe to your liking, or to a lesser form of pain. But it is art formed but what is given to you, the pliable material the shit of life, there is no new invention, but a suicide note sung to a different melody, or a yelp of joy thrown back to earth by the padded cell made of clouds. I am escaping from hell but every time I come out, I am thrown back in by well-meaning people. The only light I enjoy is in the act of escaping, because I can never have escaped. I am trying to adjust sanity to my requirements but it is making me mad. You can't make sunshine blindly, or clouds out of concrete.

Maybe art is there for people to express their madness. The presence of beauty in a human mind will make anyone go mad. And being loved when you don't think you are worthy of that love will make anyone go mad. That anyone was me.

I was drowning and tried to grab Sarah's hand without realising she was drowning too. Because of the stress of overwork, the constant discrimination we faced, and certain Creative Routes members bitching about Sarah because she wouldn't indulge their self pity was getting to her and she was becoming unwell also.

117

But we were still able to have our good times too. On Valentines Day we and other members of Creative Routes participated in a protest march organised by the artist Aidan Shingler. It was called the Kiss It! March. Kiss It! as in kiss my arse – the one you keep injecting. It was protesting against traumatising and emotionally obliterating effects of forced treatment. The Kiss It! flyer quoted from Article 5 of Universal Declaration of Human Rights, which states: *'No one shall be subjected to torture or to cruel, inhuman or degrading treatment or punishment.'*

Rude staff. ECT. Disabling drugs that make you feel you are being internally tortured. Solitary confinement. Less rights than a prisoner. Is this mental health care? Holding someone down with force and puncturing skin intrusively with a liquid that will turn your own body into a straitjacket, doesn't that sound like rape? And if you were to force ECT on someone without the context of psychiatry, isn't that torture?

The march left Whitehall Place and composed of mostly survivors but more poignantly than that were the families of those who didn't survive after being restrained. Rhythms of Resistance, who are a wild and colourful bunch of drummers lending energetic percussion to protest marches and direct actions, were there too. Our very own Creative Routes drum circle banged away too. I didn't have a drum but a placard saying, 'Stop the Pricks'. We all wore sticking plasters the shape of an X on our buttocks, not a target to inject but an indication this is where you should kiss, government and psychiatry. It was lovely weather and a triumphant atmosphere. Every government building and hospital we passed we paid our respects by bending over and showing them our arses. A Valentine

Card was also given to 10 Downing St. I didn't get to sign it but I wanted to personally thank the government for fucking me without my consent. We ended up at the Imperial War Museum, the ex-site of Bedlam, and had parties, and picnics and music.

We also went up to the Mind Harrogate in March to provide workshops and entertainment. The stress of it was unravelling my relationship to Sarah. I thought she didn't care about me anymore. I felt like I had no skin, a brutal sensitivity making even the sweetest breeze burn my being. I was increasingly psychotic. Couldn't see that Sarah was hurting too. We didn't know how to help each other. We worshipped each other but ended up tormenting each other. I wanted to be looked after. I wanted a loving parent to hug and protect me, and give me a happy childhood. And I was looking for that in my partner Sarah, and become angry at her for not providing it. It is not her responsibility to do so. It is mine and mine only to be nourished and to love myself. If I can't find ways of loving myself, how do I expect people with their own problems and issues, to do that to me?

This acknowledgement made me realise my childhood was still damaging me. I had forgiven my father but conditioning of neglect and brutalisation touched the core of my being. Where there should have been love there was fear. I lost hope in myself. Depression set in. Couldn't see the light. All I could see was the one thing in the world I love with all my heart was about to leave me. Thoughts of suicide started to creep in. I was on the razor clouds of paranoia. I thought I could teleport, tried to kidnap god, and smashed CTTV cameras.

Things came to a head, a head that wanted a gun to be put in the mouth of it, when we did an event called 'Celebrating Mad Culture' at City Hall. I gave a speech as to what Mad Culture was. I said,' *It is a celebration of the creativity of mad people, and pride in our unique way of looking at life, our internal world externalised and shared with others without shame, as a valid way of life. It is an acknowledgement that we are reacting to a society that is scared of us and will hijack our art and literature once our artists and writers are dead and therefore deemed safe and easy to control, corrupt and capitalise. Our culture is that we have control of our lives without being brutalised by a psychiatric system that wants us to conform to an ideal of normality that doesn't exist anyway. It is challenging the idea that madness is something to be hidden; it realises that visibility counts in order to break the stigma that has a stranglehold over every single mad person alive today. Mad Culture is saying, 'Yes, yes!" to life even if embarrasses the 'normals'.*

Mad Culture is saying: I won't hold your sanity against you. My reality is good enough. Is yours?

We are already an alienated sector of society, in fact the most alienated sector of society. We are not full members of this society or culture and that is not going to change without us changing it. Because why is it in their interest to change what makes them feel comfortable and superior. So in that sense we need to create our own culture in which we feel comfortable in. Some would argue that leads to separation, but we are separate. Where does madness fit in 'normal culture'? We are the untouchables. Only fit enough to work in sheltered workshops, to be cleaners, media scapegoats and to paint multi-million pound masterpieces. Put simply, in this present culture we have victim status; in our culture, we are just ourselves. WE want a culture that doesn't produce a suicide every 40 seconds.

Why have pride about suffering distress, some may say? It's not about that. It is pride in our strength to survive that distress and what it teaches us, and not to feel like lesser beings because of it, and to question why we feel lesser beings because of it, to question that madness is an illness and not a human response to a sick society, a sick upbringing.

Can you imagine a world without music, art, dance and drama? It would be an empty, bland place. So why is the world without your music, art, dance and drama? If life is a stage, is yours worth watching? What would make the show better? Can we change the ending? Or make it a better story? Culture is letting us tell the story not them – it is as simple as that.'

My heart was not in the speech. I didn't believe my own words anymore. It made me feel like a hypocrite. There I was talking about pride in being mad but if I was able to give up my insanity in that moment, I would have. I had succumbed to self-pity. I was a chaos ghost consisting entirely of broken glass turmoil. One of the most painful aspects of madness is that wall that goes up when you are ill. It hasn't really been talked about in literature. Sylvia Plath called it the Bell Jar, that sense of being cut off from the rest of the world. You are behind something that removes you not only from the human race, but the rest of the world. The sun doesn't shine – it's only there to burn you if it can get through the barricades of serrated transparency. And it's only transparent at first glance because if you look hard you can see it. You can see the disconnection, you feel it like a crucifixion, and the transparency just means the precision of the agony of a drowning person can be seen through a ocean wave of psychosis drowning you to if you try to enter it to save the person, unless you know how to swim and very few people do. Some psychiatric medication can slow down the waves but you are still in the water with the sharks.

It is a protective device – the person behind it is in a fear which is out of this world, so out of this world you must go. It is a road block to the soul. It is a road block to the end of the road.

Sarah was at the point of exhaustion at the event. She could barely stand up. I told her to go home and sleep and not to put everyone first before her. 'They are not babies, y'know!" I yelled at her. "Don't tell me what to do!" She countered. That was the last time I saw her face to face for about two months. We had split up.

It had to be done, because we had come to the point where we were just hurting each other, and needed a break from each other to sort our own heads out. This couldn't have come at a worse time, the physical agony I endured because of my gallstones made it extremely hard to maintain a mental equilibrium. I was constantly depressed and kept slipping into the psychotic sunshine to be burnt. I was not an easy person to be around. I remember one time going to the GP to request a stronger painkiller than what was available over the counter. The locum I saw took one look at my list of 'conditions' on the computer scene and said, "Could the pain not be psychological?" He refused to prescribe me a strong painkiller on the grounds that I might overdose on them. It said on the screen that I had a history of self-harm and attempted suicide, and that influenced his decision not to give me painkillers. I wasn't suicidal before I went into the consulting room but I did feel something along those lines when I left it. So because I was mad I had to suffer the physical pain.

After 7 months on the waiting list, I was finally called in to have my operation on the 29th of March. The nursing staff were lovely, offering me kind words and human comfort. What a shocking contrast to being on a psychiatric ward. When I was on a psych ward later that year, I told one of the horrible nurses about my experience on the ward during my op and asked why psych wards couldn't be the same, especially when that comfort was the very thing that was needed and treasured by patients. "Oh, we can't do that. That means giving the patient what they want." "What do you mean?" I asked. "If we did that we would be rewarding people for inappropriate behaviour." I was so shocked at that. Instinctively I knew that was the case, but to hear it from the horse's mouth, scared me. To think that this reward and punishment mentality was still alive and well in the mental health system, and comfort was anathema.

I was on the Nightingale Ward at St Thomas, and my bed overlooked the river, a comfort and a serene entertainment. The other people on the ward were also having a cholecystectomy, which involves removing the gallbladder using small incisions. The next day after the op, my stomach felt like it had been kicked in by a horse. I couldn't sit up and when I eventually got out of bed I walked to and from the toilet at a 90 degree angle. All of us on the ward walked like this. We all looked silly but it was dangerous because laughing caused the most pain! My blood pressure was a cause for concern so I was kept on a drip until one hour before I was discharged. I wasn't ready to leave – I couldn't even bend down to do my shoelaces but they needed the beds so there were a lot of people leaving the hospital walked at a 90 degree angle. Directly after my op, I had noticed my thoughts were becoming even stranger. My GP surmised this was because of the anaesthetic, which can trigger psychosis in vulnerable people. Jesus, I was as vulnerable as you could get.

Recovering physically from my op meant staying at home listening to my mum moan about her various aches and pains, and telling me how to live my life. I was utterly heartbroken by my split from Sarah, just had an op, and was a prisoner of a nagging mum. Don't forget I was already psychotic and paranoid too. I meet nobody socially any more. Loneliness is a horrific mental illness. Believe me, you can die from it. I was dying from it...

The air I was breathing was hurting my broken heart. Breath is always colourless, and now my heart was too. The break-up was nobody's fault, I know now, though at the time I thought it was because I was so fucked up, that nobody could love me.

I didn't think I was real anymore. I thought I was someone else's dream. I would say: 'what are you thinking, the person who is dreaming me? You dream to release pain and I am the person to feel it. My being is forgotten by you once you open your eyes. Where do I go when you stop dreaming?'

Melanie, my beautiful friend, texted me every day even though I knew she was struggling with her own shit too. My love for her developed, deepened. But I still wanted to die. I went to Clapham Junction Railway Station to recon the site of my planned suicide. Pam's, my CPN, heart is in the right place but everything they offered was just spitting on a raging fire.

Pam arranged for two members of the Home Treatment Team based at Lambeth Hospital to assess me. I didn't want Home Treatment. I didn't like the idea of being forced to take medication in my own home. It also offered other rudimentary home 'treatment' such as help with shopping and self-care. When the two of them knocked on my door and began by telling me that Home Treatment was for very ill people and that I did not fit the bill 'because my personal hygiene was good and my shoes were clean(!)' They continued to make basic false assumptions about mental health like that. They were **telling** me I was not suicidal when in fact I was. They said this because I wasn't crying. They didn't let me talk and I didn't want to confide anyway because you could see there was no way I could tell them anything. They had their minds already made up. They had an aggressive swagger about them which scared me. I could just imagine them holding me down in my own home to inject medication into me. I am an old hand in the psychiatric game but their behaviour shocked even me. If I had been just in the first phases of mental distress and suicidalness and was hoping that the medical services could save me, and had what I just experienced as their first contact with mental health services, I would have waited till they left and committed suicide. But the best was still to come. I told them that I couldn't sleep and that I had just split up with my partner and it was very painful. One of them perked up and said, "Well, kill two birds with one stone and read Mills & Boon at bedtime and you'll be fine."

The hole the relationship break-up had left me with was shattering; I wanted to die and for him to be as blasé as that, I couldn't believe what I was hearing. What scared me was that I was totally vulnerable and they couldn't see that. Then he kept referring to my partner as he/him when I said it was a her.

Home Treatment on paper is such a good idea in that people don't need to go into hospital. But if the same kind of staff is manning Home Treatment teams as inpatient wards, it just means being abused in your own home. I said to Pam afterwards "If that is Home Treatment, I'd rather go into hospital." I said that because I didn't want memories of being unsafe and traumatised in my own home. At least, in hospital, the association wouldn't be so personal once I got out.

What happened instead was I did get a kind of Home Treatment care plan but it wasn't peopled by Home Treatment! I had the CPNs of my Mental Health Centre in Streatham visited me or call me once a day to see how I was doing and to gauge my level of suicidal intent. Or I would go to the Centre to see someone. They were lovely. I was well looked after and I felt that they really cared for me and wanted the best for me. They tried to get me to go to the Women's Crisis

House in Streatham instead of hospital. I went for an assessment there and didn't like the vibes of the place. It was cold, quiet and clinical even though homely decoration was the intent. I was interviewed by one of the therapists. There was just no warmth from this woman, just icy analysis of my whole personality in an hour interview. I declined the offer to stay there. I learned later that the Crisis House has had two suicides in only its year long history.

I can't sing my praises enough for how the staff of Streatham Mental Health treated me when I was ill. I was listened to, treated with respect, and spoken to like an equal, and a real genuine warmness. I remember one of them, when I told her about the Mills and Boon comment and homophobia of the Home Treatment guy, she said, "Report the bastard!" Which gave me my first smile in weeks, for lots of reasons I guess, that she cared about me, that she wasn't homophobic, that she saw the mental health system needs improving, and didn't take sides with a fellow nurse.

I have thought about this since then, and I realised if every mental health job was filled by passionate, kind, intelligent people like her, the system could be changed overnight. And the service user experience would be changed overnight.

My psychiatrist also referred me to the Picup clinic at the Maudsley to tackle distressing psychotic symptoms. Picup stands for 'Psychological Interventions Clinic for outpatients with Psychosis'.

So what is CBT for people with psychosis? Well, their website says this:

'CBT is a psychological therapy designed to ease distress from emotional problems. It is widely used in the NHS as an intervention for a variety of problems such as depression, anxiety and obsessive-compulsive disorder, and more recently, psychosis. CBT works as an adjunctive therapy to medication, and it is not recommended as a replacement for medication. CBT works on the 'here and now', and assumes that unpleasant emotions are closely linked to certain thoughts or beliefs about the self eg. 'I'm worthless'. Such thoughts also tend to lead to maladaptive behaviours, thereby setting up pernicious vicious cycles. Therapy involves identifying these unhelpful thoughts and behaviours, and gradually attempting to understand them, test them out, and hopefully change them. Therapy also involves changing maladaptive behaviours and trying out new coping skills for dealing with distressing experiences such as hearing voices.'

My therapist was a kind, warm woman and she helped me make maps of my thinking. Just seeing down on paper that my thoughts follow a set course every time was a revelation. Negative thinking is not merely seductive, it is a road made of quicksand. You will be swallowed up by it if you give any weight to it. Believe it or not, negative thinking is not who you are fundamentally, who you are deep down. Because the real you can watch it and change it. It is something you are taught to do and if you have done it for a lifetime, the groove goes deep, it's etched on your bones. CBT – or anything that focuses on the positive - is one way of recreating another groove. It is not easy - but in identifying how my thought processes followed a pattern that fed and gave psychosis its sustenance, I could see the road I was about to travel down. CBT gave me a crossroad to choose from, and I choose positive thinking and action, even though it was easier to water the terrible and beautiful flower that is psychosis. Here is an example of one of my psychotic maps, one that tried to chart how I believed people were clones: It usually began with a sense that people have a different energy about them, a negative aura that means there is something to be scared off, which leads me to ask myself: 'why are they like that?' Because thinking people are clones has been a reoccurrence when I am unwell, that is where my thinking automatically goes. In our CBT session, the therapist and I tried to find the root of this thinking, of how it began.

One possibility was that there was a time when I was a kid and left home alone with the TV on. I remember there was a film that had a profound affect on me. It was about aliens coming into human's homes when people were alone. Because I was only about 4 and alone, I couldn't separate TV fantasy with reality, and I thought they were coming for me. In the film, they managed to infiltrate humanity as clones. It could also be that I have always have felt like an alien myself, that I don't belong in this world. So when I ask my people have a different energy about them, I usually come up with the serrated proposition that they might be clones. This makes me feel anxious and scared of people, so I withdraw and my behaviour changes and my discomfort shows. People react to that and *they* act differently towards me. This then becomes proof to me that they know I know they are clones otherwise why are they acting weirdly.

One thing I learned in CBT is that madness is quite logical. If it were illogical, it would be a different manifestation every time and relating to nothing in the real world. But there was a method to madness, and connections to the real world.

My psychotic map with regards to auditory hallucinations is also a set path where I've walked a 1000 times before. I see the imprint belongs to me, because it is there, it is easily to fall into. Usually it starts with me beginning to feel detached, which comes from the unwelcome genesis of poor sleep and interpersonal stresses. Then my concentration starts to go and in turn the voices I hear increases. Because it feels it comes from the outside of me, I perceive that I am losing control, and I get scared, very, very scared. I withdraw from people. This withdrawing from people is the pivotal point where the psychosis can be stopped in its tracks or is the point of no return. If there are no people around you, it is hard to reality test your perceptions. If you can't hear or see them, you can put words in their mouths and actions that don't belong to them. And if you remove yourself from the social arena, your friends and people who care about you won't be able to see your deterioration and say those few kind, warm words that will confuse your paranoia and make you question it. So the CBT help me see at every stage where I could put a spanner in the works. When I see I am beginning to withdraw, I force myself to go out. I still find it hard to talk to people or ask my friends for help. But it is something I am working on.

Slowly with this kind of support I came out of my low point, the dark room of paranoia was beginning to let in light day by day. I saw again the colour that life has and the beauty of it too. But one day I got a letter that plunged me and tore me into razor blackness again. I didn't believe light existed, and it had never existed. That is mental illness. You can't deny the fact it harms your soul when you are in it. And even 15 minutes before psychosis kicks in you were in a totally different world.

The letter was from the benefits office and it stated they believed I had made a fraudulent benefit claim. They believed I was earning and lying about having a mental health problem. The letter was harsh in tone and made all sorts of threats. It said I would have to attend a tape recorded interview with an investigator where I would be under caution. Caution! As I reread the letter again, my heart went into overdrive and flapped wildly like sheet in a maelstrom. Tears came. It seemed they found me guilty when there was nothing to be guilty of. I wasn't earning, doing lots of voluntary work, yes.

The best milieu for fear is darkness. Just imagine hearing a monster locked in a room with you. You hear it. It is sneaking up slowly on you. Your fear comes from the fact you can't escape, and is further compounded by the fact nobody else sees this monster. So you think they are on the side of the monster. Just from the fear, you want to enter an even darker room, that of death. Death may have its monsters too, but the few seconds of respite between life and death seem worth losing your body over, a body that contains hell that knows how to smile.

My first instinct was to call my CPN. Hearing how upset I was, she asked me to see her straight away. When she read the letter, she was shocked at the tone of it and grabbed the phone to speak to the guy who wrote the letter. It was the first time I saw Pam angry. She told him I had just been unwell and that the way the letter was written was extremely dangerous to vulnerable people. She said if I had been suicidal when that letter arrived, it could have been the thing that pushed me over the edge. She was right. If I had been paranoid and suicidal when I received that letter, I probably would have walked into oncoming traffic. Pam tried to reassure me and promised one of the nurses at the centre would come to the interview with me. That did help reassure me. But once I got home again, I wondered who would possibly report me to the DSS for earning when I wasn't. A couple of days later, someone threw eggs at my door and shoved shit through my letterbox. The paranoia I was trying to keep at bay took over me like a skin disease. I was convinced the whole world was against me and wanted me dead. I was convinced the next thing to happen to me was petrol and lit match through my letterbox. I peered out of my window and I was sure the vehicle across the road was a surveillance van from the authorities; they wanted to kill me. Luckily, I had a CBT session and she helped me to regain some perspective. I was still scared but I stopped the psychosis from growing into something unmanageable and dangerous.

So after about five days after receiving the letter, I calmed down a bit and got less paranoid, but still the voices giggled every time I looked out of the window as if to suggest they knew somebody was spying on me.

When I met my friend Fiona in Camberwell, I bumped into Sarah. I asked if I could hug her; she nodded yes. I did so and whispered in her ear, "Please look after yourself." It felt so good holding her in my arms again. We began talking to each other and she supported me through the rough time I was having with the DSS.

The day of the DSS interview came and a CPN attended it with me. The investigator tried at first to intimidate me. But I was so indignant it didn't have an effect. In fact, I let him have it. Am I being punished for wanting to help my mad brothers and sisters? What's this bullshit about social inclusion when this is how you treat people who try to do good? Well, if you can do voluntary work why don't you go and get a real job, he insinuated. Because I don't know ahead of time when I am going to be unwell. If you could find me a paying job where I just go in when I am well, please do.

The CPN with me nodded in agreement and added that my voluntary work was part of my care plan to improve mental well being.

A few weeks later I received a letter in which they accepted the work I was doing was therapeutic and I was left alone again.

Now Sarah and I were speaking again, I resumed my work with Creative Routes again. My first job was as bus conductor!

Previously, during one of our midnight chats, Sarah came up with the idea of using a double decker bus as a 'chariot of desire'. She thought it was a quotation from William Blake. While we were talking, I looked the poem up on the internet and had to break the news to her that the line went: 'Chariots of Fire'. "Ah well, we'll corrupt it – we're mad."

Pete, a drummer with CR, and ex rock and roll musician, suggested in the tradition of the Merry Pranksters of the bus called 'Further' we would Christen ours with the destination 'THERE'.

We had the bus for four days in total. We stopped off at The Maudsley for the first three days. The best part for me was our impromptu drumming session down that long dismal corridor of The Maudsley. We kind of had permission... I think. We shook up that hospital. There were 20 of us with assorted drums and we entered the corridor from the back of the building. BOOM BOOM! A nonplussed security guard tried to stop us but he was no match for 20 nutters with drums! He got swallowed up by the insane seismic tide. We paused at every ward for a minute's drumming. Usually a face would appear at the meshed window on the locked door to smile. One woman kissed the glass in appreciation; Sarah kissed the glass back. That was Sarah's favourite part of the three days. We also paused at the door to the ECT room to give it a good kicking.

We spent the afternoon on one of the grassy areas inside the hospital and drummed for some of the patients. Most of them couldn't leave and had their noses pressed against the windows. A few who were allowed out came and joined us in the drumming.

Another one of our stops was Peckham Fire Station. We drummed on the front forecourt for a little while. The BBC were filming us, and on camera Sarah got to ask a senior fire officer about his experience of entering an inpatient psychiatric ward whenever a patient smashed the fire alarm, triggering their response. Sarah recounted one of her experiences on the ward at the Maudsley: she said none of the firefighters would look at her; they would look at the floor. She said the fire alarm was set off so somebody from the outside world would come in and enliven the brutal, emotionally cold locked ward. But they refused to make eye contact. This senior firefighter bravely admitted he was scared of the inpatients. He also couldn't connect that the people in Creative Routes who were drumming outside his fire station were the same kind of people that stayed in that sort of ward. This is why organisations like Creative Routes are important in showing the rest of the world all the sides of our experience.

It was quite a hot day so the firefighters turned on their hoses and sent a jet of water down on us to cool us down. We rounded off the day by going to Blake's Vision, a wall mural dedicated to Southwark's own visionary.

Most of the time on the bus was driving around, giving Southwark residents either musical entertainment or a headache. The majority of people we passed on the street gave us a wave, a couple told us to shut up and gave us the finger. One guy who was pruning in his front garden threw a rose onto the opentop upper deck.

The third day we were knackered. The combination of hot weather and hours of drumming had taken its toil. So we only did one circuit of Southwark before heading South to the seaside. It was decided we would go to Brighton but ended up instead at Littlehampton because of the backlog of traffic coming out of Brighton. It was one of those bright, sunny hot days in England where you can't see a single grain of sand or a pebble for the human swarm. It was the first time I had been to the seaside for a couple of years and I gorged myself on ice creams under the hot sun. On the way back to London, we drummed through a retirement village. We must have sounded like the horsemen of the apocalypse; I hope we didn't give anyone a premature heart attack!

While I was away from Creative Routes, the BBC got in touch with the organisation to do a documentary about mad people. They decided to call it 'I Love Being Mad' and they also interviewed other mental health stalwarts like Rufus May and Aidan Shingler.

They filmed us on our bus following the route of chaos, and a music concert where Sarah conducted with bananas. Sarah wanted to tackle the subject of ECT in the film so it was arranged that she met an ECT 'expert' on film. Sarah estimates that she has had over 70 ECT 'treatments'. Her memory is decimated. She doesn't remember half the life she has lived. I haven't had it but to see the pain and horror it brings up in Sarah has made me passionately anti-ect.

Because of my work with Creative Routes was based in and around Southwark, I would go to the Maudsley quite frequently for meetings. Sarah and I would spit at the ECT door in disgust that it was still used in a supposedly progressive hospital.

One day Sarah and I were walking that long dismal corridor of the Maudsley when Sarah flinched when she saw a new ECT sign was stuck up on the wall. The old sign had been nicked by Pete, a Creative Router. I looked up and down the corridor to see if anyone shared it with us. We were the only ones, so I wretched the sign off the wall. Sarah, Gem and I quickened our step to make good our escape. Suddenly out of the ECT door, two nurses came out. Shit, I thought. They paused right next to the wall where there was just a shadow on the wall instead of an ECT sign. Shit, I thought again. Shit, thought Sarah. I'm hungry, thought Gem. The two nurses gave us a glance. Had they seen the sign in my hand? I pushed Sarah faster down the corridor. Save yourself, I told her. I foresaw a wrestling match with the two nurses. But they didn't follow us; they went into a different door.
Phew!

Sarah and I talked about stealing the actual machine, smashing it up and replacing it with flowers. This was about the time Munch's The Scream was stolen. I wrote the press release for the time we would steal that evil machine. It went:
'Munch's The Scream was stolen recently. We are doing our version of it, stealing the silent scream, and the screams of psychiatric patients are silent. Or maybe they are just ignored. The painting has a high

worth to it. What about the worth put on human rights, and memories that are gone forever? Loss of memory is a very common effect of ECT.

So this is the deal: we will return the machine if the Maudsley returns the memories lost in its ECT 'treatments'.

But we never did get a chance, maybe one day... I may go to jail but that is a lesser punishment than the knowledge that this thing is still used. Sarah said it always felt like a punishment to her, castigation for being mad. In any other context, that machine would be seen as an instrument of torture. Just because it has a psychiatric use, it is moral to use (!) When you further question what psychiatry is and how flimsy its premise, then ECT is an absolute travesty of human rights.

We are fighting with forgotten memories. We can protest lost memories but if you can't remember what you've forgotten, you can't prove what you've lost.

The BBC filmed Sarah returning to the Maudsley where she had been strip searched, and had forced ECT treatments. An ECT 'expert' was found to be the counterargument to Sarah's concerns about what ECT did to her. Of course, I love her to bits so I am biased but I was astounded by her strength in facing a thing for her past that is nothing less than a torture to her. How would feel if you had to face a machine that wiped memories from your being? What are memories but your life? How does it feel not to have the full quota of your life lived? How would you feel if you came face to face with a professional who thinks it is a good thing to send electricity through your brain and steal some of your mind? With her quirky, original mind she came to the ECT room with Madeleine cakes. This was a funny but poignant gesture. If you read Proust's masterpiece 'In Search of Lost Time', you would get the joke. In the book, the main character bites into Madeleine cake and all his memories come rushing back. Sarah can eat the equivalent and it brings back nothing but holes in the fabric of her life. She handed the ECT man a cake. He got the reference straight away. He was cold and clinical about the ECT procedure. The only warmth or excitement you hear in his voice is when he talked about newer procedures. He seemed annoyed at Sarah's humanness and fear of ECT. I was in the waiting room while Sarah was filmed in the 'treatment' room with him. The look of pain and horror in Sarah's eyes at being there was compounded by bizarre presence of a Laura Ashley catalogue in the waiting room. Fucking Laura Ashley! If this was the Maudsley's answer to what the average poverty stricken service user would like to read, good god, they will never get it.

Sarah felt that ECT was a punishment, abuse of mad people. The only welcome thing he said was that the use of ECT had declined significantly. From once doing hundreds a year, the Maudsley now gives about 40 courses of ECT a year. But still it's 40 too much. The expert said if there wasn't ECT some people who stopped eating or drinking, or who were grossly suicidal would die.

That well may be, but at what cost to those who it hasn't helped, to those it has traumatised, to those who have lost human memories, to those who feel it has stolen their personality, to those who committed suicide after ECT treatments?

When the filming was done, Sarah stepped into my arms. She was shaking and her clothes were soaked through with sweat. It took her over a week to get over the experience.

It was about this time I was making my own documentary too, inspired by an idea by Chris Fitch. I had meet Chris Fitch through First Step Trust, my old workplace. He is a sociologist who was one of the research fellows of the Living Project. The aim of the project was to document the lives and experiences of people with mental health difficulties. It wasn't a dry and academic study but wanted to describe all aspects of the experience of madness and how it affects things like housing, money, employment, education, and relationships with family, partners and professionals as true as it was able. Hopefully the findings of this project will go some way to improve the lot of the most disempowered section of society.

I heard from First Step Trust that he wanted to meet me after he read my memoir. I was beginning to realise how far-reaching that book's influence was. I was a bit nervous he would be an academic bore. My first meeting with him dispelled that assumption. He came to my house and I opened the door to him and a tub of Hagen-Daz ice cream for me. "Quick, put it in the freezer before it melts all over me!" I liked him immediately. We had a shared love of the group the Pixies and of underground films. He asked if I would make a film with him one day that reflected the issues The Living Project had illuminated. I said I would.

It was about a year before I heard from him again. He offered me the carrot of going to Edinburgh to a psychiatric conference to show the film. Edinburgh, I had never been to. But hundreds of psychiatrists in one place scared me. I asked myself things like: Will I be the only mad person there? What if some doc was getting withdrawals and was itching to section someone and I was the only one to hand? I was only half-kidding when I thought that. But I wanted to see Edinburgh and I needed to make the film anyway.

Through my Mindfull Productions tenure, I had met a lot of people who were interested in being the subject for a film like this. I contacted one guy called Stuart Adams, and asked him if he would still be interested in taking part. He jumped at the chance. He was passionate about providing mental health awareness to a hugely ignorant society. He is a lovely guy, warm, kind and articulate, and that came across in the film.

The film was aimed at mental health professionals and wanted to show that 'your' patient has a life out of the consulting room. Because professionals have a tendency to make judgements about people's lives solely based on a 15 minute appointment. I wanted the film to show how mental health difficulties can affect every corner of life, where medication can't reach or isn't effective, even simple things like answering the phone. A walk in the park is not simply a walk in the park if you are accompanied by paranoia. Along with the disabling effects of medication, depression, stigma, hallucinations and isolation, it is not a life at all. I called the film: Life As A Side Effect. One of the worst things about having a mental illness diagnosis is the aloneness it engenders. It takes you out of the picture. Is there medication for loneliness? That is why organisations like Creative Routes run exclusively by mad people for mad people are so important. Like Stu said in the film, medication 'is not a simple cure in a tablet form and all the troubles go away. If it was the whole answer, I would take my tablets and get on with life as before... it was when I met other service users that I began to tackle the underlying turmoil inside that perhaps caused the whole thing to escalate in the first place...' He also told me, off camera, that if a non-mad person had made the film it would be very different because the filmmaker would not know what the right questions to ask were and the right experiences to look into. He also felt more secure and at ease talking to someone who had been where he had been. He didn't feel looked down upon.

But the making of the film didn't go smoothly in that it didn't fit into a comfortable time schedule. Both Stu and I had our hotspots of illness so a lot of filming was delayed. In fact, I was still editing in the early hours of the morning I was meant to go up to Edinburgh.

I stayed in The Point Hotel in Edinburgh. Its website claimed it was one of top 50 designer hotels in the world. I didn't think so. To me, it resembled an East European Communist Factory haloed by strategically placed bits of neon. I had a beautiful view of Edinburgh Castle from my window though. The presentation went well, Chris said I had the psychiatrists eating out of the palm of my hand. They did seem to like me and want to hear what I had to say. But the best thing was nobody sectioned me!

That was on my mind because I was actually becoming sectionable. I was in the middle of a medication changeover. After my mental wobble in the spring after my operation, I was put on Amisulphride, but now was coming off it. I was weaned off my anti-psychotic Amisulphride for lots of reasons. Amisulphride just did not take to me; it made me feel like I owned Frankenstein's body, that I was a mishmash of surplus limbs and strange electricites. I couldn't sleep on that medication, I couldn't pee on that medication. So Dr Mcgowan, my consultant, weaned me off them. The first week was ok; symptoms were there but not enough for me to take notice.

I slip quite quickly into psychosis, frighteningly quickly. The seeds of the psychosis were germinated on that train back from Edinburgh. The train was stuck around Peterborough for hours. I was in a sickeningly hot carriage with people having panic and asthma attacks. That experience bore a blunt, hoarse flower that you get without enough water. The train company finally provided us with a coach to drive us to Stevenage train station, where a train would finally take us in to King's Cross. Maybe I suffered heatstroke on that train and it affected my mental state, I don't know, but my thinking shifted into strange...

I know I am in trouble when I am psychotic whilst I am depressed. The dark mood feeds the psychosis, and the mind can't help but choke on the meal. I was suicidally depressed for no reason I was able to recognize, although I wouldn't commit suicide because I loved too many people to leave this life. It was horrible but dealing with just the depression I could stay alive. Not so with the psychosis. I had demons stalking me. They laughed at me, made fun of me, pinched and bit into my skin, I could feel their disgusting body heat as they leered and spat into my ears to feed my paranoia. So when I see a whole army of them chasing me, I am gonna run, I am gonna want to escape. Jumping out of the window or into a busy road is an escape. No time to pause for thought, or check reality. If you could see what I saw, jumping out of a 10th floor window would be the sanest thing to do. Every time these demon hallucinations appear in my life, the delusion that humans are really clones also rears its ugly face. It starts off as a gut feeling that humans don't look quite right, they are wearing ill-fitting masks and minds. People have a different energy about them. My senses are affected: the visual and aural quality of my reality become more dream-like.

The umbilical cord that connects me to reality is fraying and festering. I want to severe the bond. I withdraw from people. Because I am scared and wary of them I act strangely with people; People react to my change in behaviour, which makes people withdraw and act strangely with me. But I am not seeing that: they are acting differently because they are clones and they know that I know they are clones. All this feeds a vicious circle, thinking becomes circular. And where do you break the circle that has no discernable beginning or end? When you are psychotic, it is harder to think, to concentrate. You don't have the mental or emotional resources to question or challenge your thinking or to analyse rationally. You are drowning with only occasional glimpses of air and sun.

Well, it was in these glints of air and sun I could see I needed help. My last episode was still raw and I remembered that I almost didn't make it. Stepping in front of a train was a walk in the park if you thought demons were going to literally rip you apart. There was still some of me to realise that I was becoming delusional and that there was not that much time left before I became totally unreachable.

I didn't want to tell Sarah how bad I was because she wasn't well, going through psychosis and low mood herself. So I shared my fears with my good friend Melanie and she didn't let me down. She outstretched her hand and stopped me from drowning. Firstly, she tried me to get to do things that would take my mind off my mental distress. But I was getting worse by the day, so when I told her I had an appointment to see my psychiatrist, she asked if she could come along to give me support and talk to my doctor. I said ok. I knew I needed a friend there to give me the courage to be truthful to my doc and not whitewash my darkening mind and the effect it was having on my life and survival. I was so touched by Melanie's offer, especially as she was struggling with her own madness and had to cross the capital from North London to reach me. She met me at Streatham Railway Station, which was literally yards from the Mental Health Centre where my Psychiatrist would see me.

We got to see my consultant Dr Mcgowan. I have to say he has been my best Doc to date. I told him I was thinking of suicide to escape the hallucinations and mental distress I was having. He suggested a stay in hospital. I said yes, I knew I needed to be in a controlled environment. He found me a bed on the Lloyd Still Ward at St Thomas's Hospital.

Melanie accompanied me to the hospital. That woman saved my life. How do you repay someone who has done that? Melanie, I love you so much, thank you for being there for me.

The first patient I 'met' was George. He was white-haired, about 5'6, mumbling constantly into his nicotine-stained fingers. It was hard to identify his accent, but he looked partly Irish. I am not one to diagnosis someone on the spot, but from experience of my dad and old age psych wards, he looked like he had some kind of dementia.

He was wearing three pairs of trousers, and stank of urine. He would pee himself and instead of change out of his soiled trousers, he would put another pair on. He had the strange habit of pouring water over himself. His socks were usually half-way off his feet. The pyjama shirt he wore was always stained. Wherever he walked he left a snail trail of spilled liquid. I did wonder what his life was like leading up to this sad pitiful end to his life. Was he ever happy? I don't know. And he doesn't know either. That's the tragedy of dementia. We were told to shut the door to our rooms so George couldn't enter and take our belongings. But a closed door was no barrier to George; he came in anyway and took things like toothbrushes and flannels. Not to keep though; they usually ended up on someone else's bed. I actually developed a soft spot for him, even when he blocked up the toilet with toilet rolls and his pants, or snatched people's food from their plate.

A nurse came to do the admission paperwork. It was a mundane and bureaucratic exercise interviewing me about the state of my soul. The nurse then showed me around the ward. We started at the nurses' station. She pointed one way, 'That's the smoking room' and in the opposite direction 'that's the TV room.' 'There's no TV in the TV room' a passing patient informed. There were a few more communal areas and finally the dining area. People were having their dinner when I was shown the area. A stout Irish woman called Eleanor said to me, "Who are you visiting?"

"No, I am here to stay for a while." She threw open her arms. I felt silly but went up to her to be hugged by her and pressed into her bosom. "It's heaven here,' she told me. You're totally off your rocker, I thought to myself.

I stayed in the dining area as it was nearly time for supper. The next person I met was also called Eleanor. She had the demeanour of a nervy school teacher, pixy looking with mousey hair. She told me she was God. It was good to see a woman who thought she was God, that women were having a better class of delusion.

She was into channelling everyone and absorbing the guilt of the universe. She was as middle class as hell, making her stick out. She told me over my food that I was kidnapped by the king of Nepal. She was too jittery for my liking and I stayed out of her way. I did give her some of my washing liquid so she could wash her clothes. I was obviously the wrong thing to do because she then suddenly turned on me, saying I was in the centre point for all the contamination of evil in the universe. I felt like it so agreed with her.

We all had our own rooms, which I was thankful for. On the aquamarine door to my room was a name plate, with hundreds of rubbed out names of people who have moved on, and some of those people rubbed out permanently because the pain was too much. Behind my newly scrawled name were names that couldn't be rubbed out, like: PROF, Frank, MIX92 FLY, LiLi, and Jesus...

The loudest person on the ward was a middle aged Greek woman. She was a figure of fun for the staff to tease, an annoyance to other patients, and a burden to her family. This is what madness has done to her, seemingly the thing that made her who she was had gone. That there was just no person behind that ravaged face was the accepted notion about her. But as I waited behind her as she clumsily made two cups of tea, her soul shone through her eyes just for a split second: she was still very much alive and still very much special. She handed the teas to the nurses who couldn't go home because of the London bomb blasts.

The next day she was back to her tortured routine and she pulled the hair of one of the nurses, screaming, "You thieving bitch, give me back my trousers, you thieving bitch!" For all the time I was on the ward, she continued to protest about her stolen clothes. I never did get down to the bottom of the mystery of where her clothes went, whether the staff or patients did actually steal it, or whether she never had them at all.

The days went by, some days had less screams than others. The only unusual day on the ward during my stay was when there was the constant wail of sirens, more than usual. St Thomas is a general hospital too. Then I got a text from my mum, saying there had been bomb blasts in London, on the tube and on a bus. Later I found out suicide bombers had detonated devices. Shit. It made me aware how detached us guys were from the outside world. We didn't seem so mad now. The detachment was ensured by the fact we had no TV in the TV room, and nurses who kept to the age old tradition alive of who could talk least to their patients.

<u>TV ROOM WITHOUT THE TV</u>

Do you know I'm here? Inside a saint.
stuck in a room on a psych ward that overlooks the
Thames
jigsaw pieces of the Houses of Parliament show
in the missing pieces that are the old trees
swaying
The windows are open
only a few inches mind
so we can't jump out of our pain
so we have to endure the TV room without the TV
so no-one hears our screams, our rants, tears,
our inappropriate laughter at a world terrorising itself
so no-one can see our journeys on a 1000 miles of
corridors
or our skin being torn in protest of a life it has to
cage and enclose.

Do you hear us? Or don't we exist?
We don't exist, I think,

because those here before me have scrawled
on the sills: 'SAVE US' and nobody has
The trees outside have camouflaged us lost people
well.

I have yet to be an inpatient on a psychiatric ward where the all the nurses did their jobs. This is what some MH nurses think their job is: Sitting slumped in a chair, looking at their nails; a patient tries to speak to them, they go deaf or release a bored sigh. Or if you are really super qualified, mimic someone's distressed shouting or screaming back at them. An arsehole called Wilbert did this when the Greek woman in question shared a table with me for lunch. She was no longer shouting, but was in fact subdued and depressed. 'Maw Wah Wha' he threw at her. "Please don't do that," she murmured, her head bowed.

But there were amazing nurses too. One called Iman, who did the night shift, she would talk with me at night, assured me. Knowing she was on the night shift, I felt protected and cared for.

Time on a psych ward is either total tragedy or total comedy - there is no in-between. Except the soul-destroying boredom. There was some exercise on offer, nothing special. I don't think our psychiatric patient exercise program will top the video charts. It was held in the dining room by Byron, a smiling Rastafarian. He brought Reggae to exercise to. I caught snatches of lyrics, such as: 'Please let me go... How do I get out of here...' The routine consisted of very basic steps, but could I get it right? Drowsy from medication and wearing my jeans without a belt because they confiscated it when I was admitted, I was all over the place. And my jeans kept falling down. One step forward, one step back was just too complicated for me, and I decided I would not come to the next session.

One morning was taken up in the hunt for the plug so I could have a bath. I went to the nurses' office; they couldn't find it. It became my adventure for the day, a bloody crap adventure I know, but anyone who has been on a psych ward will understand that you need to make your own entertainment or adventure or you will die from the ennui. The total boredom was broken up by lesser boredoms. I had sessions with Sarah, the occupational therapist, doing stuff like art and life skills, which was basic stuff and not really interesting or challenging to me. You could see her heart was in the right place but I do remember thinking she just doesn't get it, she doesn't know what it is like to be really mad or what would really help her clients. She was the mediator between nurses and patients. We would complain that there was not any toilet paper in the toilets. She would relay this to the staff and then tell us because George kept flushing the toilet rolls down the toilet, we had to ask a member of staff for a toilet roll whenever we needed it. They could not see how demeaning that was for us, especially when most nurses were annoyed if you asked them for *anything*. But I did like her.

After a few weeks on the ward, I was stable enough to be discharged. My discharge meeting was just a bureaucratic exercise. They discharged me into the 'care' of my mental health team in Streatham, without, I found out later, contacting them. I had no care whatsoever after my discharge, nobody bothering to see how I was. Three phone calls to my mental health team went unanswered before they contacted me. St Thomas Hospital overlooks the Thames, and the bridge is minutes away. I could have jumped off the bridge, and been dead for quite a while before any mental health professional saw something was amiss. According to National Confidential Inquiry into Suicide and Homicide by People with Mental Illness, (Safety First, DofH, March 2001) the majority of suicides happen on the day after hospital discharge. No surprises there. But I wasn't suicidal, just happy to be alive and back with my doggies and the people I loved.

After coming out of hospital, I analysed and dissected why I had a depressive episode that almost killed me. Using CBT and Buddhist meditation, I saw I still had feelings of self-pity that were dangerous. Although I had made huge strides in dealing with my past, I still hadn't taken **total** responsibility of my thoughts and emotions. I still justified bad behaviour and unkind words with the excuse, 'you don't know the shit I've been through'.

What I used to do and what is sadly prevalent in the 'mad' world is thinking 'I am a victim'. It is easier to blame others because it is scary taking total responsibility for your emotions and thoughts. I suffered terrible abuse as a child, rape and violence almost to the point of death, but I didn't have a choice as a child of how to deal with it, but I do as an adult. No one else can do anything about it. *Only me*. And do you know what: taking responsibility for my thoughts and emotions and not blaming others has been the most freeing thing that has happened to me.

It doesn't matter if my bitterness is justified, it is self-defeating and just adds to the shit that made me bitter in the first place. There is so much pain in this world, it is difficult not to be hardened by it. But the final outcome of that is to create more negativity, more shit, a more perfect environment for others to harden in. And bitterness comes essentially from the standpoint of 'poor little me', one borne of self-pity and not self-respect. Respect for self means you know bitterness is the wrong route to go down, that will defeat all the good things inside you.

Self-pity blinds you: you don't see the people around you for what they are. Their pain is not as good as yours, for example. But pain is not a competition. It is an opportunity to put into effect compassion for your self and others without blame.

2005 had been a tough year for me, but what it taught me was something that had the prospect of making the rest of my life beautiful.

Before I went back to my voluntary job with Creative Routes, I stayed at home and wrote a book of poetry called 'Eccentric Fish'. The opening poem of the same name went: 'Eccentric Fish – swimming in set concrete – but still making the shore – still growing flowers – still smiling in a world of endless liars', and set the theme for the rest of the book. Eccentric Fish don't drown. As we proved in Trafalgar Square.

Dave Morris of City Hall had been a supporter of CR a long while, in fact it was he who gave CR the historic opportunity to be the first performance gig at City Hall.

He must have liked us, because he invited us to perform at the yearly Liberty Festival in Trafalgar Square, London's Disability Rights Festival, hosted yearly by the Mayor of London.

The performance was to be mostly music, a small and tight set. Well, that's how it started. The wonderful thing about Creative Routes, we have a hard time understanding what small means. Call it solutions of grandeur! So it started off with five people just performing their guitar music; it ended up with 25 people, with drums, dancers, and a mad woman who strolls around the stage wondering what happened to her bedroom and it was transported to Trafalgar Square! Yes, that's right, I played the mad woman.

We had rehearsals beforehand at the Blue Elephant Theatre which were really intense. We tried to fit 45 minutes of performance into the 40 minutes Liberty gave us to perform. Nobody wanted to give up part of their own act, so tempers got frayed and the rehearsal room got heated. There were people who questioned if we could pull off our complex fusion set off at such a big gig. I never doubted that we could pull it off. I can't describe it or classify it but Creative Routes has the magical ingredient that always provides miraculous and perfect outcomes. We prove that there is beauty in chaos. I was not in the least bit worried about and those Creative Routes members that were worried looked at me as if I had bumped my head too hard when I said that.

We got someone from the Young Vic to make us some props, oversized household items to accentuate that mad people are often made to feel small. They did a great job and made us a cigarette, a hair brush, an ashtray and a plug.

On the 3rd September it was mounting chaos until we were on. Getting our stuff onto stage was mayhem. The stage managers beforehand were calm and collected. But after lugging oversized furniture, giant syringes filled with bubble bath which leaked all over the stage, a hospital bed borrowed from the Maudsley Hospital, they were muttering to themselves. Yeay, I thought we are turning the whole world mad. Tee hee!

> *Liberty*: The condition of being free from restriction or control.

"There was totally anarchy on stage, but it was brilliant!" said a member of the audience after Creative Routes under the banner of Deadbeat International played the Liberty stage for forty minutes. That is the magic of Creative Routes: we sing beautifully even if we don't know the words to the song society has written.

Klektivo, a band we had previously worked with, kicked off with their world sounds. Each act fused with the next, so Klektivo played the intro to the legendary Maggie Nichols' two impassioned songs. Maggie Nichols is a legend in the mad world. Her voice was unforgettable, elevating, raising everyone higher than poor ole Nelson on his column. She is also one of the best jazz performers on the European improvisation circuit. She did two songs, one about madness and another about the war in Iraq. Maggie's soft lines flowed skilfully into the rough edges of Stephanie

155

Something's gutsy performance of punk blues. Stephanie Something is another amazing member of Creative Routes. She has Asperger's Syndrome, so the world is a frightening and confusing place, but she has the beauty and guts to face that world, and respond in kind with her deep, honest music. Chas de Swiet's haunting violin came into centre stage next, followed by Pete MacDonald, the man behind the name Deadbeat International. Pete has incredible stories to tell about his life. He has spent most of it as a rock & roll genius. His guitar playing is untouchable and magical. I am always glad when he gives his rock and roll anecdotes, such as the time he was locked up in a police cell with The Clash. In between his time as rock musician and member of Creative Routes, he has battled with drug addiction and alcoholism, but has beaten both to be one of the kindest, funniest people I know. He is another one who has been there since the beginning of Creative Routes, and he gives the Creative Routes consistently successful formula as this: "we like to start by thinking Big, throw in a few dozen totally Unfeasables, then mix it up with a generous measure of the Practically Impossible. If any of it comes together at all, the Effect can be pretty damn near Unbelievable."

And so he proved as he played his two heartfelt rock and roll love songs, bringing the crescendo of the whole act higher and higher with an incendiary energy that shook Central London. The figures in the painting of the National Gallery facing our stage came alive, liberated from their 2 dimensional worlds.

The backdrop to all this were two films playing on a loop: the dreamlike RPM, a Creative Routes film made in collaboration with the South London Gallery, and a film made by Antonio Ribero as he followed Creative Routes on a journey to and on the Kiss-It Campaign against psychiatric Abuse and the draft mental health bill.

As Lord Byron said, "Liberty is the eternal spirit of the chainless mind." Liberty, a condition a lot of us aren't used to, especially people with mental health difficulties. We are in the shadows a lot of the time. And the darkness seems to be growing bigger in the shape of the Draft Mental Health Bill. This shadow did share our stage for a little while, but in the exhilarating, rising passion of our anthem sung and rapped – and written by - the magnificent performance poet Lloyd Lindsay, there was just no room for anything dark and gloomy.

**"This is the statute of LIBERTY
don't try to define ME"** Lloyd belted out fervently.

My role for the piece was to be a mad woman. I didn't take part in rehearsal because I don't need to rehearse to be mad, my childhood did that for me. While the music played, I wandered around the stage in my pyjamas because it is my bedroom, looking very alone and my own world. I don't notice the music through my pain. I watch TV while the world is beautiful but ignored because it hurts too much to look at it. In fact, I do more than just ignore it. I hide from it – in boxes marked madness, and medication. The last box I am in is LIBERTY. These were just cardboard boxes on stage with the words written on them. I hide under the box until the dancers came to liberate me from my box by ripping it apart. There was a rocking horse on stage, so to celebrate my liberty I rode it for a while, and then I jumped up and down on the Maudsley bed with Sarah. Gem the dog was looking as bemused as ever at the antics of the humans she loved. I had a fake ball and chain around my ankle. I took it off and exuberantly swung it around my head like a lasso, spinning faster and faster, harder and harder. Suddenly the plastic chain snapped and the huge, black – but thankfully empty – ball went flying into the audience. Luckily it didn't hit anyone on the head.

The Draft Mental Health Bill –our Fear Embodied- was represented on stage by a huge dark shadow made of wood and black sheeting. Bye Bye Fear Embodied – looking silly and senseless next to our light. So it left the stage. In fact, we threw it off. Can a mad person ever be free? Of course we can, in our creativity at least. The shackles of medication, pain, forced treatment, stigma, and poverty explode and turn to birds.

All the world's a stage. But our song, our dance, our poem, our play does not end. But has to be stopped just to let people out of the theatre. The theatre being roofed by birds in flight. How apt. We were free. We are free. Be bigger than your cage, it is your responsibility as person labelled mad.

It was exhausting being mad in front of thousands of people, I usually am mad in the privacy of my own home, or in front of a select few people. I was so tired that I didn't change out of my pyjamas to go to the Mad Pride gig in East London. I slept through the next day. I guess I need to train harder so I can be madder for longer. I think listening to a speech by George Bush ought to do it.

Through Creative Routes I was familiar with Mad for Arts, which was a media project that aimed to promote mad creativity and provide a platform for people with mental difficulties to talk about public art that inspires them. In 2004 they did a series of short films about 5 pieces of public art that inspired 5 mad people, which was shown at the Tate Modern. That was the day we got chucked out of the pub because of Gem. In 2005 they did a series of films for Mad for Poetry. A lot of people recommended to me that I do it, so I emailed them and wrote a little bit about myself and nominated Charles Bukowski's 'Writing'. When I was in my 20s I loved Bukowski, although I have outgrown him a little now. He was far-removed from an academic poet that you can get. There was no separation between life and art, none at all. His language was stark and simple, and he was looked down because of this. He said somewhere once: *'These words I write keep me from total madness.'* I knew what that meant.

Poetry or psychosis. I find it hard to tell the difference sometimes. The voices I hear dictate to me how I live my life, and at its worst how I should die. Through writing, I can fight back with my own voice. Writing – as Bukowski's poem states – 'keeps the hoards from closing in, writing stalks death'. I know I would be dead if it wasn't for writing. Bukowski taught me that I didn't have to read the script everyone else is reading – I could write my own and make the story of my life better... and I have. The book in your hands is the proof. Writing for Bukowski and me isn't an academic exercise. It is much more important than that. It is a re-shaping of a suicide note into a life story I want hear. Bukowski has definitely been my best psychiatrist.

I think writing has become too middle-class, and it is hard for the middle class to feel passion. I read what is published by the major poetry publishers and it makes me sad. No wonder it is a dying art on the page. Modern poetry is to me without passion. Oh, it is clever but it is contrived clever. I don't like poetry that says to people "Look at me, the intellectual." What I like in my reading and art is its ability to express something that every single human who has ever lived has thought and felt but never said. That's why you gasp when you see it and never forget it. That, to me, is great art.

The booklet that accompanied the series of films does say 'It's significant that none of the poems selected clings to such outmoded conventions, preferring instead to follow its own rules, establish its own reality.' The other poems selected by the four other people were 'Conceit' by DH Lawrence, 'Tulips' by Sylvia Plath, 'Oberon' by Spike Milligan, and 'Still I Rise' by Maya Angelou.

The filming was split over two days, the first day on location around London and the second day was being interviewed at my flat. It was a small crew of camera/sound person, producer and director, and they were sweethearts, good fun to be with. The first bit of filming took a while because it was shot in one of those small parks dotted around Central London. I just had to say a few lines introducing myself but I kept getting interrupted by some nearby church bells. I had to time my speech in between peals. Then we travelled around London by taxi grabbing shots on Waterloo Bridge and the Waterloo area. When we were there, we talked to some of homeless people there. When they heard about my background, that I was mad but was a poet too, I just kept getting hugs and just total love and acceptance from those guys. They were genuinely happy for me, that I wasn't homeless when I so easily could have been. I have a tattoo on my arm that says: 'Grace Beats Karma'. My karma dictates I should be dead or in jail, but I am not, I am a writer and an artist, living an amazing life.

The day of filming was finished off with me reading the poem at Muses Café, Creative Routes monthly cabaret night, at The Crypt of St Giles in Camberwell. It is a quite a well-known jazz venue and that came across in the finished film, lots of shots of candles on small round tables and poetry drifting through a haze of cigarette smoke.

The second part of filming was me being interviewed at my flat. There I said writing was necessary for survival. It was like throwing a thousand stars into the darkness. Your life becomes illumed.

I had no time to watch those thousand stars settle. No sooner had I finished filming with Channel Five, I was up in Oxford. Jason emailed me the details of a Chipmunka book launch in Oxford on October 10th 2005, Mental Health Day. Ordinarily he would have gone up himself but he was going to be in the States on holiday and asked if I would go up and give a speech about Chipmunka and read a few poems. The book was called 'FROM GOLDFISH BOWL TO OCEAN' and it was a moving collection of stories by people living with mental illnesses, describing their experiences and their lives, from the first stages of their illness, to diagnosis and eventual recovery, edited by Zoë Mcintosh. I hadn't been to Oxford before, and Zoë sounded a lovely woman, so I said okay. Nearer the time, I was told I would be giving a speech alongside Paul Farmer, then Director of Public Affairs of Rethink, and John Bird, the founder of The Big Issue. It was slightly unnerving that I was going to say something together with these public speaking stalwarts, so I didn't even bother to write or plan a speech; I was going to speak from the heart, and didn't worry any more about it. A week before the launch, I could see poor Zoë was getting stressed from organizing and nervous about giving a speech. She also disclosed to me that the night before, she had a dream nobody turned up to the launch and spoke to rows of empty chairs. This is common to everyone who has planned an event and is very natural. In one of her emails, she said a guy called Jon was going to be my PA for my stay in Oxford and was going to pick me up from the station. To identify himself, she said he'd be wearing glasses, a black woollen hat and have a Guardian newspaper in his hand. Very secret service. We decided against trading phases like 'the grass is greener on the other side.' I have to say I was slightly disappointed that it was the Guardian and not Woman's Weekly.

Jon was my PA for my stay but he was a bloody rubbish one. I told him to stand on his chair and give me a football chant when I gave my speech. He didn't. But I forgave him because he was such a lovely guy, full of heart and one-liners, and an atheist student of theology.

I stayed at Wolfson College, a large graduate college of the University of Oxford, situated in North Oxford beside the River Cherwell. My room overlooked a lake, a bridge, boats, ducks and frisky squirrels.

The launch was going to take place in a meeting room of the college. On the seats were some photocopied poems of a young man called Edward Best. I had a cursory browse of the poems. They were simple but beautiful and poignant, and made even more painful when I read that he had committed suicide after being diagnosed with Schizophrenia a year earlier. He was only 20. Oh no, I thought, another one lost, another talented, sensitive being lost. I was choked. I decided I was going to read one of his poems in his memory.

The room slowly filled up. We ran a bit late because John Bird's train was stuck outside Oxford. As it approached 7pm, John Bird finally made his entrance. The audience took to their seats and we speechmakers sat behind a table. John Bird talked first, and expressed himself passionately about how too many of us are socially engineered to be failures by a society that brings up kids without love and respect. Then it was my turn to talk. Following on from John, I told the audience I was socially engineered to be a failure by bad parenting, abuse, a school system that didn't care and punished me for being different. I talked about the time I was 14 and began to hear voices, that it was a time where society could have intervened and helped me. But what did they do? Made me worse – by chastising and ostracizing me for being ill. I recounted that I was alone and in pain for many years until I met Jason. He was the first person to believe in me. In that moment my life changed. I told them the story of a mental health professional who when I told him I was a published writer, had been on TV, and performed at The Young Vic Theatre, he wrote down 'Delusions of Grandeur'. I felt a surge of mischievous satisfaction when he found out what I said was true!

I finished off by reciting some poetry. I had been in a rush that morning, so I got a friend to print out a few of my poems. When I looked on the train what poems she printed, I had to laugh that she printed two about orgasms. The perfect material for a mental health talk. What was she thinking! I told the audience this, and one of them said, 'Go on, read it!' But I didn't. I recited the poem 'Lost and Found', which I wrote about my beautiful connection to Sarah.

It was the meeting of two minds
of 2 people that were lost
who discovered they were not
lost at all.
It was the world around them
that had gone astray
The World used maps like 'work', 'judge'
'hate' and 'blame'
These two did not like to be in those places
there was no escape except to use our
own maps of 'love' 'passion' 'art' and 'poetry'
But we were told:
'There is no place for you here. Tear up
you heart-shaped maps or we will tear
them up for you.'
So we ran away from them
followed our hearts

and
found
each
other

I finished off my speech by reading one of Edward Best's poems, entitled 'So We Become'.

The thought manifests the word
The word manifests the deed,
The deed develops the habit
And habit hardens into character.
So watch the thought and its way with care,
And let it spring from love.
Born out of concern for all beings.
As shadows follow the body
As we think so we become.

Then Paul Farmer, the then head of Public Affairs at Rethink talked and gave his support to Zoë and the mental health community of Oxford. Subsequently the floor opened up to the audience for questions and comments. The third person to raise their hand was a middle-aged woman. What she said absolutely floored me. "I just wanted to say thank you to Dolly for reading Edward's poem. Edward was my son." Tears came to my eyes, but I suppressed them. God, I will never forget that moment as long as I will live, a hugely powerful moment. Afterward, I did think: why am I still alive and Edward isn't? I still don't know. Luck maybe? I say that because I discovered later that Edward had attempted suicide twice in two days. What is absolutely horrific about it was that Edward was hospitalized after the first attempt but unfortunately – but not unsurprisingly – he wasn't cared for properly by psychiatric staff and was able to walk out of the hospital to commit suicide. He could be alive today if psychiatry did its job.

After the talk, the first thing I did was walk up to Edward's Mum and give her a hug. Then we ate but all I could do was think about Edward and his Mum. I got good feedback from the audience. I had one Oxford University student come up to me who admitted that she only came for the advertised free food but what instead happened was that her perspective on mental health had changed completely. I thanked her for reminding me on why I do these talks and write these books.

The next morning Jon and Zoë took me for a slap up breakfast in a posh hotel and wander around the various colleges. Then it was back home to London for a long-deserved rest.

A week later, I was back at work. Months previously, Sarah had contacted Mental Health Today and offered Creative Routes services to organise the creative activities and entertainment for the Mental Health Today exhibition on November 2nd at the Business Design Centre. We had a meeting with our contact, Bill Brooks, and brain-stormed and came up with packed and extraordinary day of mad originality. I gave it the name of The Madtring-a-ling-a-ling Thing.

The ideas we came up with were painting on tiles, knickers, hankies, socks. Dream postcards made so those who have lost their lives to suicide can continue dreaming. There was going to be a huge roll of paper for people to write a collective poem on the theme of who am I? There were also going to be percussion workshops and parades. My role for the day was the playing of the Wise Thing, dispensing wisdom to anyone who needed it. I had a Bedouin tent, well pagoda tent actually; camels, well Gem the dog actually. I gave the story of Gem being a camel who was rejected by other camels because she had no humps. I had a steady trickle of seekers come into my tent for advice. Some just needed directions for the toilet, some wanted the meaning of life, which I gave as Engleberg Humperdick. There were more poignant moments when people come in asking things like, "Why doesn't anybody love me?" which turned into counselling sessions.

We were really excited about the day. We thought we were going to have fun, and be an important part of the exhibition. We were wrong.

From the very moment we unpacked and set up, we had nasty little trolls from Business Design Centre security bully us from the start to finish. I just could tell they were told by their superiors to keep an eye on us mad people, their aggression was far too focused for me to think otherwise. The list of what they did to us could probably fill a good ten pages of this book, but this is what I saw with my own eyes: People asked to put their shoes on and having their shoes kicked towards them; one coming into the tent where Gem the dog was asleep beside me and being told I have to hold her lead. I told the guy she was asleep and didn't need her lead held, he got nasty and said then I am going to ask you to leave; Or when I was MCing, told to stop what I was doing. Or during the drumming workshop, where we had service users smile and bond with us, have their eyes of joy turned to looks of fear when the security guard stopped what we were doing. Or when we were taking our things out of the building and have that reception guard close the door on people carrying equipment.

The security guards didn't just bully us; they intimidated the service users taking part in the workshops, which is unforgivable. Some of them were so very obviously vulnerable. What made the situation worse, the Mental Health Today staff let this happen to us. Bill Brooks said, I am trying to make both parties happy. You couldn't make the security guards happy unless you got rid of all the mad people present. The biggest complaint was noise levels. We needed guidance as to what were appropriate levels of sound. Did we get it? No, we had the hall monitors stop acts midway or stop my MCing in mid-flow. How very ironic when we survivors talking about having our voice heard and having our voices gagged at a mental health exhibition. What was frightening Mental Health Today as an organisation paid for these bullies to treat us this way. They didn't want to take responsibility for supporting us, instead they shifted the blame saying, well, we didn't know you were going to do drum workshops and live music. Maybe they ought to read their own brochure where it states quite clearly that was what we were going to do.

I shot an angry email to Bill Brooks, part of it said: "You provided for us a disempowering experience. We will not do a Mental Health Today thing again. Some of Core Arts who have provided what we did on other years were there yesterday and they told us they have had the same problems. So here is another suggestion don't ask a user arts group to participate in the exhibition. After speaking with Core Arts and how we were treated, we felt we were a tokenistic presence. In fact, on our feedback forms that participants filled they said we were the best part of the exhibition and the only place they felt welcomed. It was almost as us as mad people were annoyance, and a lot of non-survivors would have preferred not to have us there so they can conduct the BUSINESS of mental health. And to see stalls representing organisations that have had deaths in custody as part of their mental health care was also unsettling..."

It was a Business fair and the product was our mad minds and how best to impose control on it. Can you believe there was one stall that showed a promotional video of secure units like a holiday brochure? Shame they didn't get testimonials from those who've died from being restrained. And of course you do have to restrain a person further even after they have died, because they are still struggling even though they are a corpse.

That day was an eye opener.

To say the least.

But I did encounter sensitivity, empathy and empowerment that day. We asked at reception for help with getting a couple of cabs to lug our equipment home. Of course, they didn't help us. We had to go 100 yards away to the main road to hail cabs. I went back in a cab driven by a man called Christopher

Columbus. He was months away from retiring to his Native Barbados. He had a huge laugh. He said his wife liked to box so I couldn't seduce him. "I wasn't planning to." I smiled at him. I told him about our day and about madness in general. "Ah, you guys are just the sensitive among us, don't let anybody tell you different." The whole day was worth it just to meet him.

About the same time we participated in a funding bid partly run by ITV called 'The People's Millions', where we were also treated shoddily. The basic idea behind it was viewers of London Tonight would see some short films of community groups and choose the cause they wanted the money to go to. It was a joint bid to improve Camberwell Leisure Centre where our office was based. Camberwell Leisure Centre is an old listed building with a remarkable history but badly in need of repair and modernization. It was a joint bid with Fusion who managed the building, us, and Camberwell Arts Week. It was supposed to be a partnership, but Camberwell Arts, I think, only got us involved so the mental health box could be ticked when the original form asked about social inclusion. But it was a socially exclusive exercise, and worse was to come. A camera crew arrived with a presenter from London Tonight. She didn't even ask us to get involved in the filming. Mental Health doesn't sell, she said, we will film little kiddies playing at the Leisure Centre. When we protested, she turned into a snobbish bitch. "Are you trying to tell me my job!" Well, if you are going to discriminate like that and make an already trampled and rejected sector of society feel smaller, I think I do need to tell you your job.

We could easily get disillusioned. Our saying is 'Not to Dream is Irresponsible.' We have a duty to our dreams, and I don't think I am the owner of impossible dreams.

Give me your worst, and I'll show you my best.

On the 2nd of December I made a mad dash to St George's Hospital in South West London. Sheila, my sister, was in labour. This was her second child. Her first child was delivered by Caesarean but she wanted to try and deliver her second child naturally. But it did not happen. The baby's elbow had pierced the womb wall and Sheila was rushed to theatre for an emergency Caesarean as the baby's heart started to slow down.

Mum was crying, and the rest of us stood around in a tense daze. Sheila and the baby could die.

Then little Kallum was wheeled in. He had a shock of dark hair and was a very handsome little fella. Then news came Sheila was ok too. We sighed a breath of relief and started to cry. Relief then became an explosion of joy as I held this gorgeous new human being in my arms. Life can take you to the deepest, darker corners, then in a flash be so absolutely beautiful.

EPILOGUE

So I have changed, I am a different person to the one who wrote the last book. But I am also the same person. Am I Still Laughing?

Well, what do you think, have I got a cheeky grin as I write my story?

I am a little harder around the edges. But not that much harder, and much softer on the inside.

I haven't forgotten my past. I look at photos of myself as a child. This child did not – and will not - have an easy life. I have a mind that is not usual to the norm, that causes me distress at times, but a life that can be so special. When I wrote the last book, I promised that child I'd give it a great life. I think I have kept my promise.

No one can escape pain. Nor can anyone escape the ability to learn from the pain. I am still growing. I am still in love with the world. I am still laughing.

There is light at the end of the tunnel. There has to be because you are the light. Even when you want to shut down that light and everything seems dark, something shines. It might be a tiny spark buried in an eternity of darkness, but the spark is still there to be seen, it can't be hidden. It is not in its job description to be hidden.

WAYS I HELPED MYSELF

I am not saying anything new here. Any positive person, or good psychologist or wise being will tell you the same thing.

I know some of you will dismiss this, say it is a bunch of shit. That is up to you. But not one of you can say Dolly doesn't understand. She doesn't know pain, what it is to be suicidal. I have been suicidal and have attempted suicide. I have hated myself to the point of wanting to literally rip off the skin I was wearing. The razor scars on my skin will confirm this.

Also, different things work for different people.

If using any of this helps you, great. If it doesn't help then leave it behind. Whatever you do, I wish you peace.

EMOTIONS

The world is the way today because of emotions, and how people handle those emotions. You can choose to handle them well or badly. If your parents taught you to handle your emotions badly, don't get angry with them. That is one more negative emotion to add to the pile they gave you. Be better than your parents, go further in your life than your parents. Take away power from them back to you to change your life, not that they could change you anyway.

One of my Buddhist teachers said not to resist painful emotion but peacefully co-exist with it. Don't add to it, don't argue with it, just share the space with it. After many false starts I did finally manage to do just that and what I found was that the emotion goes away that much more quickly. If you don't add fuel to it, it can't survive.

The weird thing about humans, they will pick up or be handed a piece of shit and not put it down. They will complain about the smell and pain of carrying shit but don't put it down. The measure of maturity is how long you hold on to that shit. For example, if someone verbally abuses you, how long will you carry it around with you, or add to it to make it bigger by verbally abusing in response. You don't have to take it, you can refuse to take it and pass it by in peace.

If you don't control, program, or play your mind, the world will do it for you, and the people and the worst part of the world will have the bigger effect. So let it be your own song you are singing.

Worry, fear, pain. You can see it begin and end. You can watch it and not get involved with it. So YOU are not the fear or the worry or the pain. But the way you respond to it, that is YOU-NESS of the experience.

You are not your emotions. You own them but you are not them. You can change your emotions, you can make them bigger or smaller. You can learn from it or you can not learn from it. You can react to it or respond to it.

You can punish yourselves for having emotions or you can accept that you are human, and this is how a human is – and you are a wonderful human being.

WORRY
Worry is a learned habit, not the ultimate nature of your soul. Worry takes you away from the present moment, it takes your mind into the future, making plans, imagining scenarios. If you are going to worry, use it for the time it's relevant to. Why worry about something now, about something you can't do something about *now*?
Worry is useless, a waste of energy. If something needs to be confronted, confront it. But not

aggressively, but with compassion for both yourself and the situation. Can you think of any reason not to do it that way?

Knowing that we may fail, but getting up and doing the thing anyway and carrying on, and even failing is a better attribute to being a perfectionist and never wanting to fail. Who would you rather know?

We sometimes define ourselves by what is wrong. You may do something you may regret, but are those actions going to explain your whole life away? I did a bad thing so therefore I am a bad person? Is that action going to make you a bad person from the second you were born to the minute you drop dead? Of course not.

We live in a society that depresses people. If you live the life modern society has shaped it and what it expects you to do and sacrifice for really a pittance in return, you're in hell.

FEAR

Fear is simply believing you aren't strong enough to handle what life brings you, or your issues. You are strong enough. Your amazing strength will blow you away, believe me.

If you live in fear, all those dreams you had will go unaccounted for.

What is it? Most of us live in constant fear, and only a small proportion of our dreams fulfilled. As a human being we have so much potential, so much that cries out to be done, and when we don't do them, we practice at being dead when we should be alive, and our heart loses it beautiful power. When we see others living their dreams, we want to rip them down, snatch them from the simple glory that is just being yourself. No, I can't submit to fear or not living my dreams, I do not like what I will be otherwise.

YOU ARE YOUR STORY

I have done no big thing in writing this book, this autobiography. This is my story, life story. And all our lives are lived by stories. You act out the story you tell yourself. And you can change the story. Listen carefully to the words you tell yourself. We all have a chatterbox mind. A chatterbox that has been programmed by your conditioning. A chatterbox mind that *isn't* fundamentally you. Because the real you can watch it... and change it. If you have meditated, then you know what the difference of the soul of you and your chatterbox mind. If you haven't meditated, try it out. On paper meditation sounds easy. But when you do it, you realise you don't control your thoughts, your thoughts control you.

You think 1000s of thoughts a day. You can choose to be positive or negative. The soul/mind blooms and blossoms under positivity and withers under negativity. This is a truth. This is always the case.

The mind is very clever. If it is used to being lazy, it will work very hard to be lazy! One thing we do is blame outside circumstances and people for the wrong and pain in our lives. The mind knows by giving the power for things to change in your life to things outside yourself, things will never change! So that way you can moan and complain all you want. Because people and circumstances won't change to make your life better. But why should it, if you are too stubborn to do the work yourself to change for the better, why should anybody else change to accommodate for your spiritual and emotional laziness or procrastination?

THE NEED FOR PERFECTION
Perfection is not being perfect, well, not for me anyway. If you want to be a perfectionist, I can promise the only perfection you will attain is in misery and inadequacy. Because your energy will fall into the striving to be perfect and not the art and life of what you're doing. To be in a state of constant improvement without having perfection as the goal is a much more nicer and more productive feeling and way of doing things. Because I personally found nothing killed my creativity and productivity more than the determination to be perfect. Perfection is as cold and stagnant as a statue, turned to stone in the presence of a mirror. I do not want the narcissism of the stone and perfection is self-absorbed and self-important. I prefer the beautiful imperfection of the wind that goes further than any statue; it is all over the place but at least you feel it. Slow constant positive development is much more beautiful than perfection.

Two things that have helped me grow emotionally and professional are belief and action. No more dithering. Do or don't do, don't get sucked into paralysis of procrastination. Believe that whatever your decision you can grow and learn from it. I give myself permission to make mistakes, I just don't give myself permission not to learn from my mistakes.

Are you merely a conditioned thing, and not a soul? Are you saying that your conditioning by bad parenting is the way you are going to stay? Do you want to be stuck there? I thought I would be stuck in that mode. I didn't believe I had the courage to move forward. The thought of it wracked me with fear to step into the unknown. But I so much wanted to move forward that I did challenge my conditioning. Whenever I make a step forward in emotional development, I feel freer, I feel the Dollyness of being Dolly, not what the world around me has shaped me into.

JUDGEMENTAL

Being judgemental is horrible. I have noticed something: if you are judgmental of someone – or of yourself – neither of you feel good, and is rarely productive. If someone judges you, do you grow or judge?

Being judgemental has not changed anything for the better.

So I try not to be. I challenge people, but only if I have challenged myself in the same area – and have changed in that area. If I haven't, then I can't.

POSITIVITY

You have to act on what you believe. If your mind is focusing on what's missing, you're mind is on what's missing. You are just seeing the hole. Never use a negative ruler to measure your life, it can only measure holes, you can't use it to quantify any good in your life.

You are what you think about. If you want love to be loved, you have to be loving, yes. Depressives still have egos, bigger ones than normal, believe it or not. Because some depressives want the whole world to change *for* them. 'Everyone treats me like shit.' If that's what you're thinking, then you are treating them like shit. Nobody *makes* you angry or bitter. Except yourself. The power to change can only be done by you.

But what is stopping you from doing so? The pain of habit. To step out of habit is to allow fear into your life. But everyone of you is stronger than your fear. Believe me, this can be done, once you believe you can do it. And then you do it, and the fear has been confronted and then it scariness goes, and you know what, your life and soul has just gotten that little bit bigger.

Being positive is not denying or being naïve about your shortcomings, it is understanding there is no point lingering in and punishing yourself for those shortcomings. It is asking what can I do to learn from this, what can I do to go beyond this stuckness?

Being positive is not saying all is good, that there are no problems in your life or in the world. Positivity is accepting that there are problems, but being more interested in the solution and be more focussed on that part of it.

GIVING
The more I gave, the better I felt. But I do remember getting burned by people using me because I was giving, they saw something to exploit. For a while I stopped being giving at all but that was because I

179

didn't know better, or see a way out of the problem, that I came to the realisation if you don't give me an opportunity to give and expect me to give, then you are creating a debt, and nobody wants to be in debt. So people who allow me to give, get, and those that expect, don't get.

GOALS

You need them. They don't have to be material goals, it could be something spiritual development or to do with your emotions.

KNOW YOUR GOAL. BELIEVE YOU CAN REACH GOAL. ACT ON YOUR BELIEF AND THE STEPS NEEDED TO REACH GOAL. AND STAY COMMITTED TO IT. It helps to write your goals down. Things started to change for me when I started committing to goals. For example, I felt lonely and isolated, so I created the goal of going out to social events arranged by local mental health groups. Things like that helped develop my confidence and conversational skills. It was a small goal but had huge repercussions, in that I met Jason Pegler, my publisher at one of these events.

HAVE POSITIVE GOALS, not negative ones. I don't know why, but the brain responds better to positive suggestions rather than negative ones. For example, say: "I want to have better confidence." Not: "I don't want to be lacking in confidence."

BREAK DOWN YOUR STEPS TO YOUR GOAL INTO MANAGABLE CHUNKS so you don't feel overwhelmed and disheartened if things don't immediately go your way.

This is a simple formula but hard to do, but all it takes is practice, and you will see changes within months.

MY SPIRITUAL PATH

This is not a book on Buddhism. I don't want to push my spiritual path down anybody's throat. But my Buddhism is one of the things that have really helped me.

I was brought up a Christian, but I found the hypocrisy and the notion of an anthromorphic judgemental god too much to take, so I rejected it. But the experience of materialism in our modern age is an emptying experience for me. I thought if this is all life can offer, then I thought it is pretty pathetic. I got drawn into Buddhism because the Buddhist practitioners I met were genuinely nice people, and that there was no puerile reward or punishment system in Buddhism. Nobody is going to threaten you with hell if you don't take the teachings on board.   The spiritual path is the effort you put into it. It is entirely up to you. There is no point praying for forgiveness. You do the work yourself. You forgive yourself and you learn from your mistakes. Buddhism is not doctrinal or dogmatic. It is using the teachings to reflect and meditate upon to see if it works for you.

There is no magic wand. Somebody said, Whether you think you can do something, or think you can't, you're right.

If you think you can do something, then you can.
If you think you can't do something, then you can't.

Simple. But hard to do. But not impossible.

I am Dolly Sen

Dolly Sen is a mad woman who thinks she is Dolly Sen
Dolly Sen suffers from delusions of grandeur because
she thinks she is Dolly Sen
Dolly Sen is depressed because she is Dolly Sen
Dolly Sen hallucinates Dolly Sen
Dolly Sen can't sleep, can't eat because she is Dolly
Sen
Dolly Sen is medicated because she is Dolly Sen
Dolly Sen? Is that your name, Dolly Sen
Dolly Sen is free because she is Dolly Sen

THE END

This is Madness Poem – fellow contributors:

Laura Stanton, Anton Manickam, Rob van Kranenburg,
Julie McNamara,
Patrick McManus, Anny Ballardini , Michelle Taylor,
Richard Dillon,
Heather Taylor, William Collins, Ian Davidson, Anna
Jasper, Cthulhu,
Mark Aitken, Rachel Meredith, Ronald Fraser-Munroe,
Helen Bailey,
Rachel Gomme, Jeff Harrison, Vanya Green, Laila
Elizabeth Risdon,
Laura Eldret, Zachar Laskewicz, Lauri Ramey, Sacha
Tremain,
Ebele Ajogbe, hurdy gurdy, Maureen McManus,
Timmy Jeeves
Marianna Bruggerman, Chris Hoskins, Jean Akam,
Meena Vyas,
Leah Harris, Dave Hussey, Roberto Filoseta, Sian
Owen, Steve Newton,
Alexander Johnson, James Badcock, Michael Cousin,
Jen Cendana,
Mary Krane Derr, Sara Stanton